A DANGEROUS MELODY

JANE WETHERBY

Copyright © 2020 by Jane Wetherby

All rights reserved.

No part of this book may be reproduced in any form or by any electronic or mechanical means, including information storage and retrieval systems, without written permission from the author, except for the use of brief quotations in a book review.

1

One always expects a funeral to be held on a miserable sort of day. Rain might be expected to fall in thin, drizzling lines, streaking across the lead-paned windows and rippling across the surface of puddles and ponds. Dark clouds would likely cover the sun, a rather heavy blanket over the world, ensuring that night seemed to be just moments away.

However, no one expects funerals to be held on the loveliest day of the summer, when the flowers are in full bloom and the grass is thick and soft and green. The sun hung high in the sky, which was the brightest of blues.

More morose souls might believe that the world

was mocking them, an ironic juxtaposition to the reality they faced.

Others might not even notice at all.

I, however, chose to see it as a reminder that life might have difficult days, but that doesn't mean that we couldn't still find the good in them.

"Juliana, dear, please come indoors."

I looked around and saw Father standing just inside the door to our cottage, a firm yet troubled expression on his weathered face.

"Yes, Father," I said, and followed him in through the door.

He closed the door behind us, allowing a heavy sigh to escape him. "Well, my dears, so ends perhaps the hardest day of my life."

He walked down the short hall to the dining room, pulling his tattered top hat from his head before running his boney fingers through his greying hair.

As he disappeared through the open doorway, I turned to look at the other three young women standing just inside the door beside me.

Some siblings looked far less alike than others. My sisters and I, however, looked identical in almost every way. All four of us had the same slanted blue eyes that we inherited from our father, with long, dark lashes and strong brows. Our cheekbones all sat high, a gift from our mother, and our narrow chins and pouting lips gave us the impression of spoiled young ladies when we were young but were wonderful when attempting to convince Father to spare us another sweet before bedtime.

"We should go sit with him…" said Amelia, who was three and twenty, just two years younger than I. While we all looked very similar, she was perhaps the loveliest of all of our father's children. She was a kindhearted, quiet young woman without a crass word to say. She brushed some of her pale blonde hair from her eyes, staring down the hall after Father.

"I can't imagine having to do what he did…" Isabella said. The second youngest of all, Isabella's hair was darker than my own, like the color of Mother's favorite tea.

"Neither can I," Susannah said, huddling close to Isabella, her inky blank hair nearly hiding her face. "No man should have to bury his own wife."

She was right, of course. But unfortunately, it was his duty as the vicar to prepare the eulogies of those that have passed on.

We just never assumed he would have to read of

hope and encouragement to his own daughters about his wife and their mother.

"Come along," I said, turning around and pulling the black shawl I wore more tightly around my shoulders.

Father was sitting at the head of the table, unfolding his newspaper. A fire crackled in the fireplace behind him.

I looked down at the other three, all of us unsure how to proceed.

"Father, may we join you?" Isabella asked, leaning over one of the chairs.

He glanced briefly up at her and nodded his head.

Hesitantly, we all took our usual seats.

Folding my hands together, my eyes were drawn across the table to the only empty chair. Mother's chair.

"Father..." I said, sitting a bit straighter. "I know that things are going to be a bit different now, but I think we will find a way to make do."

Father glanced at me over his newspaper, his blue eyes the very same shade as my own heavy-lidded and rimmed with pink. "I imagine we will," he said. "I have comfort in knowing your mother is no longer suffering, but I would be quite remiss if I didn't admit that I will miss her dearly."

It was as if someone squeezed my heart within me. "Yes, Father... We will all miss her, too."

He took a shaky breath, rubbing his eye. "I do wish that I could have done more for you girls. You should have been married and happy by now."

"Father, do not blame yourself," Amelia said. "How were you and mother to know that her health would be so?"

"Yes," Isabella said. "Our greatest desire was for her to be well. We thought of little else these last eight months."

"Eight months..." Father said, removing his glasses and rubbing his hands over his eyes. "I cannot believe it has been so long..."

Silence fell over us all. Through the open windows, we heard the birds singing to one another, high up in the branches of Mother's favorite lilac tree. A breeze blew in, stirring some of the stale air.

"Your mother was always the one who knew what to say in these situations," Father said in a low, sad voice. "I am going to miss her so dearly..."

He rose without looking at any of us and slowly made his way from the room, his footsteps heavy and scuffing.

He closed the door slowly behind himself and left us shrouded in the silence.

"Perhaps we should follow him," Isabella said, getting to her feet.

I reached over and grabbed her arm, pulling her back down. "There is nothing we can do for him right now. He needs to grieve, and it is possible he will not be able to if we are chasing after him. I think it's best if he is alone for a while."

"It is hard to believe that mother is really gone," Susannah said, her eyes welling with tears, her bottom lip protruding.

"I know…" Amelia said, wrapping an arm around the youngest sister and pulling her in, kissing the top of her head. "But we must be strong. For Father."

"What are we to do now?" asked Isabella.

"Well, clearly our situation has not changed at all," I said. "We are still the daughters of a poor minister. I dislike speaking so frankly so soon after mother's passing, but with one less mouth to feed—"

"Juliana," Isabella said, her eyes narrowing. "How could you say such a thing?"

"I do not say it to be morbid," I said. "But the finances that father must juggle are very tight. Perhaps, in time, he will find slightly less strain to be more of a relief."

"I cannot believe that," Isabella said, folding her arms over her black mourning dress. "Father would never wish to have more money instead of mother's presence."

"That's not at all what I meant," I said, shaking my head. "What I mean to say is that Father needs help with the finances, yes? He can barely afford to put food on the table for us all. The chickens we were able to take from Aunt Patience last summer have helped, but only marginally. What we need is to find a way to alleviate some of the finances he is required to spend."

"But how?" Amelia asked. "It isn't as if there is anything he could cut. We have no cook, no housekeeper. Mother made sure that the maid was dismissed as soon as we were all old enough to help."

"We must find employment suited for a lady," I said. "It will ensure that Father is no longer responsible for our well-being. We are fully grown women, after all. Our father should no longer have to care for us as if we were children."

"What of marriage?" asked Susannah, her eyes widening. "Some of us might still have a chance."

"Very true," I said with a firm nod. "However, as I am five and twenty, I have a far smaller chance of being chosen. And with so little to offer a man, I would have to hope that my looks alone would sway him."

"That's such a dreadful way to look at it," Amelia said, frowning over at me. "You are very pretty, sister. And you are quite sensible as well."

"Yes, of course," said Susannah. "Very sensible."

"Sensibility is only valuable to a select few men," I said.

"And those are the men you would wish to marry in the first place," said Isabella with a smirk. "Beauty is temporary, but your wit shall last forever, will it not?"

"What a kind way of insulting me, sister," I said, returning her smirk.

"But how are we to find marriage suitors?" asked Isabella. "It isn't as if we have the greatest of connections."

"What of Mr. Samson?" I asked with a shrug.

Susannah wrinkled her nose. "You mean the butcher's son?"

"He has yet to be spoken for, correct?" I asked.

"But he's dreadful," Isabella said.

"And surely he cannot be the only suitor around," Amelia said, looking worried.

"Even if he was, that still leaves three of us

unmarried," said Susannah, her shoulders sagging. Even at nineteen, she still had the manners of a child occasionally.

"Regardless, we must find some way of making connections," Isabella said, sitting back in her chair, frowning. "For if we do not, we are all destined to be spinsters, living off our poor father's measly income."

"Lower your voice, Isabella," Amelia said in a sharp whisper. "You don't wish to shame our father, do you?"

"Of course not," said Isabella, folding her arms. "But we cannot stay here, can we?"

"No," I said. "And I think that the very best option we have is to ask for help elsewhere."

"And who is going to help us?" Amelia asked.

I turned and looked at each sister in turn. "I thought that would be rather obvious," I said. "We shall ask the one person in our life who has the means to provide us with any sort of help."

Amelia's eyes widened. "Oh, sister. You cannot mean—"

"I am willing to swallow my pride in order to ask for help," I said, raising my hand. "Not that I have much to be proud of. And don't you think that I realize how much I might regret this decision?"

"I am already regretting it, and we haven't even asked yet," said Isabella, rubbing her face.

"We do not have a choice," I said. "If anyone has the capability of helping us, it will be her."

Amelia bowed her head. "For father, I suppose we must do what we have to."

"Precisely," I said. "So, are we all in agreement?"

Susannah glanced over at Isabella, who was quite pale indeed. Amelia's brow furrowed as she stared down at her hands folded in her lap.

"Father needs our support," Isabella said. "Now more than ever."

"I agree," Amelia said. "No one will be able to take the place of Mother, but we can do our best to make this transition easier on him."

"We must do our part," Susannah said. "And I suppose that will mean difficult things to come, won't it?"

"It very well might," I said. "All right, very good."

I reached over and took Amelia's hand in mine and squeezed it.

"Do not lose heart, dear sisters. We shall get through this. Our grief shall pass, and we will be able to find joy once again. Our lives are only beginning, and Father will surely do all he can to encourage us to succeed," I said.

"But how can we go on without Mother?" Susannah asked, tearing once again.

"We must trust that we will be with her again one day," I said. "Just as the good Lord has promised. Just as Father talked about this very day."

Susannah nodded, sniffling.

"We shall do it," I said. "And we shall do it together, just as we always have."

"Yes," said Amelia.

"Indeed," said Isabella.

"All right," said Susannah.

I nodded. "Very good."

2

My Dearest Juliana,

What a pleasure it was to receive a letter from you! It came at a very opportune time, as the grief of losing my dear sister has been too much for me to bear. Hearing from one of her cherished daughters has brought me great peace and reminded me that not all is indeed lost.

Things here at Templeton House have been rather busy as of late. Sir Hayward has been gone to London for some weeks, attending to business, and I had not felt well enough to join him. I am grateful that I was home when I was, as I would have been heartbroken had I missed my own sister's funeral. It fills me with sorrow to write those words, my dear Juliana. I imagine it will for some time.

As for your request, you and Isabella would be more

than welcome to come and visit at your earliest convenience. It has been some time since I have had the pleasure of your company, and I would love to share stories and news with you.

Is your father well? I can imagine this time is rather difficult for him. Please give him my love and let him know that it is Sir Hayward's intention for us to pay his respects upon his return. I know traveling is quite difficult for him with his responsibilities at his parish, but please let him know that whatever he needs, we will do our best to provide.

I look forward to your arrival and will be awaiting it anxiously.

Yours,

Aunt Patience

I looked up from the letter, the sway of the carriage lulling me back and forth.

"How many times are you going to read that letter?" Isabella asked me crossly, her gloved hands clutched tightly around her shawl. It was a rather blustery day, and even the ribbons tied around our bonnets weren't quite enough to keep them stationary.

"I just wanted to be certain of something," I said, folding up the parchment and tucking it inside my cloak once more.

Isabella's eyes narrowed, so much like my own it was almost as if I were looking into a mirror. "Certain what, exactly?"

"Her wording," I said simply. I turned and stared out over the landscape, the lush green summer hills rolling past.

It wasn't long before Templeton House appeared. Situated on a little knoll surrounded by a large front garden and an orchard behind, it was quite a splendor in comparison to our little cottage we grew up in. Where Templeton House had many rooms and very few children, we were squeezed tightly inside our little home, yet were quite content all the same.

Nevertheless...Templeton House was rather magnificent to behold, and place we had all spent a great deal of time in as children.

The carriage pulled up right out front of the large front doors.

Lady Hayward, or Aunt Patience as we knew her, was waiting out front beside her lady's maid and their house butler.

"Oh, my dear children," she said in her boisterous way, throwing wide her arms as we were helped down from the carriage. "How I've missed you."

She embraced each of us in turn, which was quite expressive, even for her.

"Are you doing quite all right?" she asked. "With your mother's passing, I have been worried sick about you girls. Just positively sick."

"We are quite all right, ma'am," Isabella said.

"Yes, we are comforted by the knowledge that she no longer suffers," I said.

"Well, at least we can know that, yes," Aunt Patience said. She looked above us, watching the clouds roll quickly by. "Come along, girls, let's get you out of this wind. We are sure to get rain."

She ushered us inside, and her butler helped us by taking our shawls.

"Thank you very much for sending your carriage," I said. "It was a very kind gesture."

"Of course, my dears, of course," she said.

We turned and headed down the hall toward the drawing room, out footsteps echoing off the long, wide hallway.

I stared up at the portraits as we passed, long lines of family members of Sir Hayward, all of them bearing a resemblance to him.

"My heavens, Isabella. That skirt. How long has it been since you mended that hem?" Aunt Patience asked.

"Oh, well…" Isabella said.

"Oh, listen to me," Aunt Patience said. "You've had a great deal too much in your mind, haven't you?"

"It is something that we will be more aware of in the future," I said before Isabella could respond in protest. I could almost feel her seething from where I stood.

We stepped into the drawing room, and just as I always was, I was incredibly impressed by all the lavish furnishings and décor.

Sir Hayward, a baronet, was quite well respected in our small portion of the country. His eyes fell on our dear Aunt Patience when she was just sixteen, and they were married within a year. She married much younger than my mother did, who was quite a bit less lovely than Aunt Patience had been in her youth. Mother always told us that looks alone were enough to sway a man, yet they were not everything.

"I see that you had the wallpaper refinished," I said, looking up at the walls as we took our seats on the sofas in the center of the room.

"Yes, indeed," Aunt Patience said. "I suppose you would not have seen that, would you? I had them changed just before my sister fell so ill…"

I was not surprised that the subject of my mother

kept resurfacing. Aunt Patience and Mother were the two youngest sisters in their family and had been very close growing up. When they both grew up and were married, they still remained close, but their relationship was a little more strained due to their very clear differences in station. Aunt Patience married well. Mother married our father, and while I believed they were happy, I could not deny that their lives were much more difficult than my Aunt Patience's.

"Would the Lady care for some tea?" the butler asked from the doorway.

"Yes, thank you, Mr. Williams," she said. "Perhaps that will take some of the chill out of these bones of mine."

He bowed himself from the room.

Aunt Patience turned her sharp gaze onto us, looking back and forth between the two of us. "My gracious, I still cannot believe that she's gone. To die so young from something so terrible…"

Isabella lowered her head, her bottom lip protruding.

"These last days must have been very hard on you," Aunt Patience said, reaching over and laying her hand atop my own. "Your mother always had such high hopes for you girls. It is such a shame that she will never be able to see you grow and have families of your own."

"Such a shame indeed," I said.

"And your father?" Aunt Patience asked. "I know I inquired about him in my letter, but what of his condition?"

"He does his best to go about his tasks as jovially as he can," I said. "To be quite honest, I cannot help but wonder if there is the smallest amount of relief in his heart. Mother was not the sort of woman to lay in bed, and I believe it was hardest on him of all to see her that way."

"No doubt," Aunt Patience said. "She always did have a great deal more gumption than I did. I always admired her for it."

She spread her hands out over her skirts, sighing heavily.

"Well, now... Your letter seemed rather insistent that you needed my help with something," she said. "What is it that you would have me do?"

I glanced over at Isabella, my heart beginning to tremble like a rabbit caught in a trap. Now that the moment had arrived, I found myself wishing that I had written more in the letter. It wasn't as if I was ashamed to ask for help, but I feared the repercussions of asking in the first place.

"Perhaps I am impertinent to ask in the first place, but…" I saw Isabella's eyes widen, clearly shocked that I decided to begin so frankly. "Since Mother has passed, Father is going to be quite busy from now on. With his busyness, it might be very easy for certain things to be delayed or forgotten about all together." I gave Aunt Patience an apprehensive look. This was quite a bit more difficult to say than I thought it would be.

"I think I understand what you are trying to ask," Aunt Patience said, pursing her lips. "You are seeking my help in order to find you suitable matches?"

Isabella nodded fervently.

I was surprised she understood me as well as she did.

"There is no fear in asking, my dear," Aunt Patience said to me with a smile. "You are going through a great deal in your life right now. It is only natural that you would be seeking ways to make a change. I believe you are correct, after all. Your father is a very busy man indeed, and his obligations to his parish might easily overshadow the needs of his daughters. Not that he would ever mean it to happen, mind you. Your father would never choose to leave you in want. However, a woman gently reminding her husband to do things, such as locate suitable matches for his daughters, is one of the many hallmarks of being a wife."

The door to the drawing room swung open once again, and Mr. Williams entered carrying a tray laden with tea and small sandwiches.

"With your mother gone now, that gentle reminder will be absent, and your father may forget his duty to you as your father to find you matches. In his grief, he may find it difficult to think of anything aside from her for some time. And yet, none of you are growing younger."

I shifted uncomfortably in my seat. As the oldest at five and twenty, I was far older than most women when they were married. Even Susannah, who was just nineteen, would seem older within a year or so.

Mr. Williams set the tray down in front of Aunt Patience, passing her a cup and filling it with tea for her.

"Now, a disadvantage I see is that you, Juliana, should have been married years ago," Aunt Patience said. "Two lumps of sugar please, Mr. Williams. And just a splash of milk."

He obliged.

"Not that I can truly blame your situation on anyone in particular, but your mother should have tried harder to find you suitable matches while she was alive," Aunt Patience said, lifting her teacup to her lips and sipping delicately.

A small burst of frustration rushed through me like a gale of wind. "Well, I believe that Mother did the very best by her daughters," I said. "It was a little more difficult to introduce us to suitors when she and Father were trying to ensure there was enough to eat."

Isabella's eyes widened. Perhaps it was a bit out of line for me to say so openly, but I would not allow Aunt Patience to dishonor my mother so easily, regardless of the fact that she was her sister.

Mr. Williams passed me a teacup. Though he did not make eye contact with me, I knew that he was likely made uncomfortable by my flippant comment.

"You are quite right," Aunt Patience said in a quiet voice. "I apologize for such a remark. Though I hope you know that I meant no harm by it."

My face burned, and I held the teacup in my hands without drinking anything. "I do know that," I said. "And I apologize for allowing myself to be so easily swayed by my own emotions. I will not allow it to happen again."

"Your mother was a wonderful woman," Aunt Patience said. "But her stubbornness left me worried for her. Our father told her over and over again what sort of life she would have if she were to marry for love instead of for money. Tried as I might, I attempted to convince her to choose a different match. I told her to think of her future family, and how it might affect them if she were to choose a man for affection alone…"

I glanced over at Isabella, who narrowed her eyes. I could tell she was cross as well, now.

"My mother loved my father dearly," Isabella said. "And isn't that all anyone could want from life?"

"Love has its place, certainly," Aunt Patience said. "But look where it has left you girls. None of you have made proper matches, and for some, it might be too late to do so." She gave me a sidelong look.

"I am well aware of this," I said. "It isn't as if I have anything to offer a man in the first place."

"You are correct about that," Aunt Patience said. "And I do not say that to be hurtful in anyway. You are aware of the circumstances in which you all have found yourself. Your father's profession is honorable, perhaps more honorable than any other. However, it is also very humble and does not give any of his daughters the means to be given a great deal by him upon their marriage."

"Then what are we to do?" Isabella asked. "Are our circumstances so bleak, no matter what we do?"

Aunt Patience shook her head. "No," she said. "For you have an Aunt that loves you dearly and wishes to see you succeed. I have a great deal of connections, and I intend to help you."

"You do?" Isabella asked.

"How so?" I asked.

"Marriage?" Isabella asked.

"Calm down, dear, calm down," Aunt Patience said. "Juliana, you are a remarkable young woman, but I imagine that your younger sisters will have a better chance of finding a husband, as they are still of decent marrying age."

"But who would take us when the eldest is yet unwed?" Isabella asked. "Is it not improper to seek the affections of a younger sister?"

"It is quite different when the eldest sister is already spoken for elsewhere," said Aunt Patience.

"Spoken of?" Isabella asked. "I thought you said she couldn't be married."

"It isn't that she couldn't," Aunt Patience said. "It's just more unlikely is all."

"So what do you suggest?" I asked. "Shall I find a position somewhere? Perhaps someone is in need of another maid. Perhaps in your home here, Aunt Patience?"

High spots of color appeared in Aunt Patience's face as she realized how perfectly serious I was. "My heavens, no," she said. But then a contemplative look crossed her face. "Though perhaps you might be onto something there..."

She glanced across the room, and her eyes fell upon a piano on the opposite side, tucked away beside the window.

"Juliana, do you still play piano?"

"Every day," Isabella said. "Though I suppose not since Mother passed..."

Aunt Patience stared long and hard at the piano before turning her gaze back to me. "Well, perhaps music might be your best option for finding employment," she said. Her face brightened. "And I might know just the place."

3

"Now, don't forget to smile. You do share Amelia's lovely smile. Kindness and patience shall be the hallmarks by which they describe you," Aunt Patience said.

"Yes, ma'am," I said as I stared out the window at the countryside passing by.

It was less than a month later when Aunt Patience had written to me, informing me that she had found gainful employment for me some ten miles from my father's vicarage. This pleased him, and he seemed all too eager for me to pursue such a worthwhile opportunity. He insisted he did not wish to stand in my way, though he did admit that he wished I could have found a husband as opposed to a job.

Either way, I found great relief in knowing that I would no longer be a burden to him. I knew it would not be long before I yearned for the presence of my sisters, but they all were quite supportive of me, and I believe that Aunt Patience's discovery for me gave them all hope that things would turn around for each of them.

"What is the name of the owner of this estate?" I asked Aunt Patience as the carriage meandered along the road at a leisurely pace. "I apologize, but I seem to be forgetting at the moment."

"Well, now, that won't do, will it?" Aunt Patience asked, folding her hands, her gloves clutched tightly in a fist. "Let's see… Well, Mr. Thorne is to be your employer. Your task is to provide piano lessons for his youngest daughter, as her governess is overseeing a great deal of other responsibilities. You shall be practicing with her every day. Mr. Thorne has informed me that you shall have your own space and will be able to have the same access to the house that the governess has."

"I see," I said. "All in all, it seems to be quite the advantageous find. How did you know Mr. Thorne was in want of a music instructor?"

"A dear friend of mine," Aunt Patience said rather simply. "By the name of Miss Waters. She is first cousins to Mr. Thorne, and it seems their daughter has quite the ear for music but no one to properly teach her. Her father is insistent that she have proper tutelage, and that was when you came to mind. He is to pay you a small salary and has freely allowed you a place to lay your head at night, and meals will be provided."

"I am quite honored," I said. And that was the truth. In actuality, I knew there was very little I could offer aside from my music to this family and having any sort of care was in some ways an improvement to my situation. Having meals provided was a great relief, as I feared I would be responsible for that, as well.

Even as grateful as I was, though, I found myself quite nervous the closer we drew to our destination.

"Now, Mr. Thorne was all too happy to accept you as I told him that you were the perfect match for his daughter," Aunt Patience said. "I informed him that you are the oldest of four sisters, and that you had quite a hand in raising them. He seemed pleased when I said that, despite your less than desirable status, all four of you have turned out to be fine young women of society."

I truly did appreciate my Aunt's help, but her

flippant tongue sometimes was enough to make my skin crawl.

"Ah, and there it is," Aunt Patience said excitedly, pointing out the window of the carriage. "Northington Park."

I turned to stare out the window myself and was impressed by the size of the home at the end of the tree-lined lane.

If I had ever considered the home Aunt Patience and Sir Hayward lived in to be large, this home was very nearly the same size. Made of weathered stone, the home itself stretched outward into two long wings, flanked on either side by dense forests. A large pond was situated along the front lawns, and lush gardens sprawled along the front of the house. Ivy crawled up the walls, and overall, the place had an air of peacefulness about it.

My heart skipped. I had never imagined Northington Park to look quite so majestic.

"Here we are," Aunt Patience said. "Now, remember everything I've told you. Keep your chin up, wait until you have been spoken to, and please, above all, my dear, keep your wisdom to yourself. At least for the time being, yes?"

"Yes, ma'am," I said.

The coachmen helped us from the carriage and

bowed to Aunt Patience as we made our way toward the doors.

"Don't be nervous, my dear," Aunt Patience whispered to me. "You are going to do just fine here."

I wished I had the same confidence she did.

"Ah, Lady Hayward," said the man at the door. "Please, come in."

The butler was significantly younger than Mr. Williams was, but his face was kind, and his thick moustache made me smile.

"Thank you," Aunt Patience said.

"Good afternoon, Lady Hayward," said a woman in a plain, grey dress just inside the foyer. Her dark hair was pulled into a tight knot behind her head. "We are pleased to have you with us here at Northington Park."

"It is a pleasure to be here," Aunt Patience said.

At once, I felt severely underdressed. Though the woman's dress was plain, it was well made and fitted her well. The hemline was lovely, and there didn't seem to be a wrinkle on it.

I always felt underdressed compared to Aunt Patience's more vibrant dresses, with their lacey sleeves and ribbon adornments, but now I wished I had allowed her to give me one of the dresses that my eldest cousin no longer wore. Anything would have been better than the simple beige dress with tattered hems and a well-worn wool traveling cloak over it. I removed the bonnet that I wore, the same bonnet I'd had for the last several years and held it self-consciously in my hands.

Even the servants wore clean, pressed black dresses with pristine white aprons. I wondered how many times a day they changed them in order to keep up appearances.

"My name is Miss Brown, and I am Miss Elizabeth's governess," said the woman, inclining her head toward us.

"How wonderful to meet you, Miss Brown," Aunt Patience said. "This is my eldest niece, Miss Honeyfield."

Miss Brown's green eyes twinkled behind her round spectacles. "Indeed. Welcome, Miss Honeyfield. We are quite pleased to have you here. I am certain that Miss Elizabeth will be overjoyed when she meets you."

"Thank you very much, ma'am," I said with a small curtsy.

"Come with me, I will introduce you to her. She is currently studying her Latin vocabulary in the school room," Miss Brown said, turning and making her way down the hall of the western wing toward a staircase leading upward.

Aunt Patience gave me an encouraging nod, and we followed after.

The house itself was lovely. There were more rooms than I could count as we climbed to the first floor, and I knew that it would be some time before I became used to it and was able to find my way easily enough. I caught sight of a magnificent library, a sizable drawing room, and a parlor. Everything was exquisitely decorated, with silk wall hangings, tall vaulted ceilings, and large windows that overlooked the magnificent views of the front garden and pond.

We turned a corner, and some new sound caught my ear. The sound of music being played.

"That would be Miss Elizabeth," said Miss Brown. "It's a rather rare thing to hear her play on her own. Perhaps she wished to impress you, Miss Honeyfield?"

We turned into a room at the end of the hall, and I nearly let out an audible gasp.

This school room was nearly as large as my family's whole ground floor. A large, ornate fireplace stood against the wall to my right, which was unlit due to the warm, inclement summer temperatures.

The windows had all been thrown open to allow a breeze inside.

A large table filled the center of the room, and the most beautiful piano I had ever seen sat in one corner nestled between two windows, ready to be played.

A young girl with curly blonde hair sat at the bench, pressing individual fingers down upon the ivory keys, her legs swinging.

"Miss Elizabeth?" Mrs. Brown said. "Miss Honeyfield is here to meet you."

Miss Elizabeth turned her face toward me, her eyes round and wide.

"There we are," said Miss Brown, stepping into the room. "Come over here so that we may introduce you properly."

Miss Elizabeth didn't move for a moment.

"It's quite all right," Aunt Patience said. "You remember me, don't you, dear? Lady Hayward. I came to visit you just a few weeks ago."

The young girl glanced briefly at Aunt Patience, but her face paled as she turned her enormous eyes back to me.

Miss Brown's smile still firmly in place, she took another step toward the girl. "Come now, Miss Elizabeth. We don't want your new tutor to feel slighted, do we?"

Slowly, Miss Elizabeth swiveled around on the stool and slid off down onto the floor.

Her curls bounced as she walked over toward us.

She stood at Miss Brown's side, coming up to her elbow. Miss Brown wrapped an arm around her shoulder, pulling her in more closely. "Miss Elizabeth, I would like you to meet Miss Honeyfield."

"How do you do?" Miss Elizabeth asked, performing what seemed to be a very practiced curtsey. She didn't smile, though, and she didn't look at me as she performed it.

"I am quite well," I said. "It is an honor to meet you, Miss Elizabeth. I hope you know that I am greatly looking forward to—"

But Miss Elizabeth's attentions suddenly seemed to be directed elsewhere. She turned and wandered over to a shelf along the wall beside the fireplace and pulled a book down. She sat down where she stood, curling up her legs beneath her, and began to read.

"My deepest apologies," Miss Brown said. "She is so very young."

"It's quite all right," I asked. "How old is she, if you don't mind me asking?"

"She will be eight next month," said Miss Brown.

"She is quite tall for her age," said Aunt Patience.

"Indeed she is," said Miss Brown. "We have been working a great deal on her social graces as of late. She has not quite matured at the same rate as other young girls her age have, and Mr. Thorne says that she is simply learning at a different pace than other young ladies do."

I watched as the young girl focused intently on the page she read, her brow furrowing. Was she doing her best to pretend that we weren't in the room with her?

She did seem rather aloof for someone her age. By the time I was eight, I had been caring for my younger sisters, the youngest of whom was two at the time. I helped with the cooking, the cleaning, the errands to town for necessities...

"She is extraordinarily gifted," said Aunt Patience. "Isn't that right, Miss Brown?"

"Indeed it is," said Miss Brown. "Which is something that Mr. Thorne would very much like to encourage in her."

The more I heard about this Mr. Thorne, the more I wished to meet him. I was to be teaching his daughter, after all.

"Well, why don't you play something for Miss Brown, Juliana?" Aunt Patience asked. "I am certain that she would enjoy hearing what you will be teaching young Miss Elizabeth?"

"Oh, well, I have nothing prepared," I said, glancing nervously up at my aunt. Why would she think it wise to put me on the spot in such a manner?

"I would very much like to hear you play," said Miss Brown. "It need not be something complex. Music is something that the Thorne family loves dearly."

My heart was caught in my throat as I stared over at the piano. "I suppose I could try something," I said.

The piano was polished and beautiful. The bench was dressed with silk, and the keys were worn, but not overly so. The piano I was so used to playing at home had long since worn down from years of pressing down on the ivory. It was evident just by glancing at it that this piano wasn't played nearly half as much as mine back at Father's house.

I laid my hands on the cool keys, and a shiver ran down my spine. I never imagined I would play in such a setting and with an audience.

"I shall play... the song of the crane," I said.

Just as I did every time I played, I did my very best to push the whole world out from my thoughts.

I didn't wish to have any distractions, and it was the best way for me to ensure that I played well.

It had been some time since I had played for anyone that was not my family. I had played a few times during church on Sunday mornings, especially when the organist was ill. And I could only remember ever playing once for Aunt Patience when we were visiting her at her estate once.

"Isn't she just wonderful?" Aunt Patience said to Miss Brown.

"Yes, she certainly seems quite talented," Miss Brown said.

"She has been playing since she was a little girl," Aunt Patience went on. "Every time I would go to visit them, she would be playing her piano off in the next room. It always helped the house to feel so joyful."

I tried my best to not allow their conversation to fill my mind, but it was difficult when they stood directly behind me. My finger slipped on the key, and it caused my heart real pain to miss a note. Flustered, I pushed on.

"Does she have experience instructing her sisters?" asked Miss Brown.

"Oh, yes, indeed," said Aunt Patience. "She not only gave them lessons, but she also has given lessons to the people in her father's parish as well. Haven't you, Juliana?"

I was just about to look up when another pair of hands rested against the keys beside me. A much smaller pair of hands.

I glanced over and saw Miss Elizabeth had slid onto the bench beside me, her hands waiting on the keys.

I continued to play, and not a moment later, she began to play right along with me in duet.

"Well, would you look at this?" Aunt Patience said with a wide grin.

Miss Elizabeth didn't say anything as she played along with me. The song of the crane was a relatively easy song to learn, though I was surprised that she seemed to know it as well as I did. I would have thought it was a song that only poorer families learned as a means of entertaining their children.

"Very good, Miss Elizabeth," Miss Brown said.

I tried to hide my smile as we played the final notes of the song and couldn't contain a small laugh when she added her own flair to the end by adding a few notes. "Well done, Miss Elizabeth. I'm quite impressed."

She blinked up at me, her large eyes a lovely

blue-green, like the ocean in the summer. "You play quite well, too," she said.

I smiled at her.

"I think this is going to work out quite well," Miss Brown said.

"Indeed it is," said Aunt Patience, giving me a firm nod and a smile. "I think it is going to be positively wonderful."

4

Shortly after our time in the school room, I was walking Aunt Patience to the door with Miss Brown.

"You have a wonderful gift," Miss Brown said. "I think Mr. Thorne was right in choosing you to be her music instructor."

"Thank you very much," I said.

We reached the foyer, and the butler was there waiting to see Aunt Patience out.

"You have everything you need?" Aunt Patience asked me as the butler helped her to shrug her cloak back on.

"I believe so, yes," I said.

"Whatever you might need, don't hesitate to ask," Miss Brown said. "Mr. Thorne is very agreeable, and

I am certain it would not be too much of an imposition."

"Within reason, of course," Aunt Patience said. Then she smiled genteelly at me. "Don't you worry about your father. Your sisters shall look after him. And I shall look after them, never you worry."

"You are too kind, ma'am," I said.

"Nonsense," Aunt Patience said. "I shall write to you soon to see how you are settling in."

"I look forward to it," I said.

Miss Brown and I waved at the carriage as it made its way down the drive, the horses trotting along happily.

"There now, I daresay your aunt was an answer to our prayers," Miss Brown said as we turned to return indoors. "I was very nearly at my wits end with Miss Elizabeth. You see, I don't have much experience with music, nor much talent. But it seems to be the one thing that Miss Elizabeth seems to enjoy the most. I was the one who suggested we seek another tutor for her, one who could focus on music more frequently with her."

"Well, I certainly hope that I will be able to meet your expectations, Miss Brown," I said.

"You have already surpassed them," she said with a smile. "Come. Why don't I show you to your room? Mr. Gibbs has already taken your belongings there for you."

My face turned pink. "All right, then."

We made our way up to the third floor of the manor. I expected us to continue even higher, toward the servant's quarters, but Miss Brown turned down the hall and stopped at one a short ways from the stairs.

"This is to be your room," she said with a smile, gesturing inside.

I stepped up to the doorway and peered in.

It was a much larger space than I had envisioned. Going to work in a manor, I had expected to be placed in something akin to a closet or perhaps something even smaller. I imagined I would have to share a room with someone else, as well.

"Is it to your likings?" Miss Brown asked.

"It's wonderful," I said, stepping inside. "Never in my life have I had a room to myself."

"'Tis true when one has sisters," Miss Brown said with a smile. "My room is just across the hall, and further along down the hall is the housekeeper's quarters. If I were you, I would do my very best to stay out of her way. She does not like to be disturbed while she works."

"I see…" I said.

"Well, I shall leave you to it," Miss Brown said. She pulled a small, silver pocket watch from a pocket in the front of her dress. "It is nearly time for Miss Elizabeth's arithmetic. She will be undertaking a test today. I daresay she will be quite distressed come dinner."

"You may inform Miss Elizabeth that arithmetic was never my favorite subject, either," I said. "But I learned it was quite useful as I grew older. It is useful for many things, including how to balance a budget, though now that I say that, I can imagine that a budget is of no interest to a young lady, is it?"

Miss Brown smiled. "Perhaps not. Though I am pleased to see you are in agreement with me about the value of her education. It will certainly help us to be able to work better together."

"I agree," I said.

"Dinner shall be served soon," she said. "And I shall see you down in the school room by seven tomorrow morning?"

Seven? That was far later than I was used to beginning my day. "Certainly," I said.

She nodded. "Very good. Have a wonderful evening," she said and stepped out of the room.

I turned to stare around the room. It was hard to believe it was all for me.

My bed was situated in the middle of the room, which to me seemed unnecessarily elegant. It would be far better to slide it to one side so that another bed could be brought in and set up along the opposite wall. There was a wardrobe along the wall with the door, as well as a fireplace with a mantle. Side tables sat on either side of the bed, with candlesticks and a box of matches. Fresh linens had been spread across the bed, which was easily twice the width of the one I slept on at home.

It was lavish and far more space than I ever had in my life and had ever expected to have.

And in a sense, it was rather lonely, too. Every night since I was a little girl, I had shared a room with someone. As each sister was born, they would all come take turns snuggled up in my bed at night.

It would be strange not sharing stories with Amelia at night.

I noticed a small writing desk in the corner, and my heart skipped. Well, at least I would be able to easily keep in contact with everyone back home.

Ten miles hadn't seemed all that far when Aunt Patience had first told me about Northington Park, but now, I knew it was quite a ways away by carriage, and it was not going to be a distance I could travel soon.

A heaviness settled over my heart, and I tried my best to find some hope somewhere deep inside of me.

I reprimanded myself for not being grateful to find myself in the situation in which I did. I was quite fortunate to be here, especially when I knew there were a great many more people who would have been floored to have received this position in the first place.

I was not ungrateful, but I would be lying to myself if I did not admit that it was going to take some time getting used to living in a new place, all alone.

The trunk that I brought with me had once belonged to my mother. Amelia insisted I have it. I thought it might be better for all of them to have it, as a way of remembering her. Amelia told me that we all had our ways of remembering Mother and that she would want me to have something like this in order to help me to transition to my new life.

I hefted it up onto the bed and opened the lid, staring down at the few belongings I had brought with me.

I lifted out a few books, some of my favorites. One of them was filled with songs that I thought Miss Elizabeth might enjoy learning. They were songs that my mother had played with me when I was about her age.

I set the books on top of the desk and then curiosity lead me to open the desk up. I discovered some other books, some spare quills, and a fresh bottle of ink, still sealed. There was even a red wax candle and a small seal. When I lifted it to look at it, an ornate letter *T* was carved into the golden stamp. An official seal of the Thorne family, it seemed. That was a kind gesture and would certainly make sending letters from the estate much easier.

I unpacked the few sheets of parchment I had packed from home. I had not wished to take too much from my father or my sisters. It would surely be much easier for me to come by than it would be for them. I set down my favorite quill beside my parchment.

I returned to the trunk and pulled out the few dresses that I brought with me. I ran my thumb over the thin, dulled fabric. It was fit that I would be spending a great deal of time with the other servants of the house, as my dresses would not be any more suited to serving as the governess's help.

I did not wish to be ashamed the clothes that my father had worked so hard to provide for me. I had stitched them each by hand, and I was proud of their quality. However, the circumstances in my life were making it clear to me that I might need to save some of the salary I would be receiving in order to purchase appropriate fabric for dresses I could wear here at Northington Park.

It was rather quiet in the house for so late in the day. I took a seat on the edge of the bed, staring out the window at the sprawling gardens behind the house, of which I had a perfect view.

Life had certainly changed drastically within the last few weeks. I had known that this change was necessary, but to experience it was another thing entirely. I had expected I would have been able to take it in stride, and I believe I had... except for when I was alone and my thoughts were able to wander without distraction.

I spent some time rearranging things in the room as I liked. Nothing would likely ever make it feel less cavernous to me, but I certainly did prefer the bed up against the wall as opposed to the middle of the room. I set my mother's trunk at the foot of the bed, ready for whatever I might find to fill it with.

I was just arranging the dresses in my wardrobe from most presentable to the least when there was a knock on my door.

I spun and folded my hands in front of myself. "Please, come in," I said.

The door swung inward, and a rather stern looking woman stepped inside.

"Miss Honeyfield?" she asked in a deeper voice than I expected. She planted her hands on her wide hips, her chestnut hair pulled back in much the same way that Miss Brown's was.

"Yes?" I asked, suddenly frightened.

"Where have you been? Dinner was served nearly ten minutes ago, and I was informed that you never appeared," she said.

I could only stare at her. "I was never informed—"

"It is your duty to remain informed," said the woman crossly. "You will not be catered to during your time here at Northington Park."

"I never expected to be," I said. I curtsied. "My deepest apologies, Miss—"

"Mrs. Frampton," the woman said, her already narrow eyes becoming like slits. "Yes, we haven't had the pleasure of being introduced yet. Though I must admit, I heard you were quite the amiable young woman, but this first impression is truly something to behold."

"My deepest apologies," I said. "I will be going to dinner at once."

"In that?" Mrs. Frampton asked. "You are to meet the master of the house, and the dress you have chosen is not only dirty, but it is far too informal for meeting him for dinner."

"But I have nothing more formal," I said.

Mrs. Frampton sighed, shaking her head. "Well, at the very least, go to the water closet down at the end of the hall. Wash your hands and face. Perhaps he will excuse your sorry state due to it being your first day here."

Without another word, she turned and excused herself from my room.

I did not have time to be cross with her. I hurried down the hall and found myself in the nicest water closet that I had ever been in. If this one was as nice as it was, I could only imagine how glamourous the ones that belonged to Mr. Thorne and Miss Elizabeth were.

I made my way down to the dining room, which I had only passed briefly earlier today. The manor was so large that I nearly lost my way, taking a wrong turn down the eastern wing before quickly correcting it and making my way over to where I was expected.

My heart was in my throat as I stood at the door.

"There you are, Miss Honeyfield," said Mr. Gibbs, the man who had greeted me at the door earlier this morning. "We have been expecting you."

I attempted to compose myself, knowing there was nothing I could say that would make up for this impropriety. And to have happened on the first day of my employment... What an impression I will have made.

"Are you ready?" he asked.

I nodded. "Yes," I said.

He pulled the door open and stepped inside.

"Miss Honeyfield, Sir," said Mr. Gibbs, bowing and gesturing to his side.

Quickly, I walked into the room, careful to keep my gait steady and smooth.

"Ah, there you are. I was beginning to think I was mistaken about the day of your arrival," said a man's voice from across the room.

I curtsied as deeply as I could. "Mr. Thorne, I am terribly sorry for my absence. I have no excuse that is worthy."

"It is quite all right," Mr. Thorne said. "It is your first day, after all. I cannot expect you to know how this household operates all at once. You may lift your head."

I did just that. When I looked up, there was a man much younger than I expected sitting in the seat at the end of the table. He was quite tall, with broad shoulders and a wide jaw. His nose, slightly crooked, was pointed and narrow. His eyebrows were thick and the same honeyed shade as his hair, which was as straight as silk and pulled back at the nape of his neck. His eyes were not at all the same shape as his daughter's, instead deep set and narrower, though even from where I stood, I could see they shared one similarity, which was her eye color.

"Come, Miss Honeyfield. Why don't you sit with us?" he asked.

Miss Elizabeth was sitting there at the table with him, at the seat beside him, her large, round eyes fixed on me as I approached.

I was not exactly surprised to see that I was the only one joining Mr. Thorne and Miss Elizabeth at the table. Part of me expected that it wasn't common for the help, not even the governess, to not join the master and his daughter for dinner, even if she was likely part of the family.

"Please, have a seat," Mr. Thorne said, gesturing to the chair across from Miss Elizabeth.

I glanced up and down the table as I sat like he asked. I had never seen such fine furnishings. Everything seemed to be of the highest quality, especially the food.

I looked up at Mr. Thorne, realizing I had feared that his words had been more of a threat than a request. But I could see that my fear was misplaced. I had nothing to fear from him.

"So, Miss Honeyfield," said Mr. Thorne as one of the servants along the wall brought a plate and set it down in front of him. "Are you finding Northington Park to your liking?"

"Oh, yes, sir, very much," I said. "Your home is wonderful."

"Very good," Mr. Thorne said as he began to cut his pheasant. "It always pleases me to hear that my staff are happy here. I hear that Miss Brown showed you around today?"

"She did, yes," I said.

A servant set a plate down in front of me, and I was grateful that the light in the room was dim and warm, for my face became quite flushed. I had never been waited on in such a way, and it felt strange for me to sit there and enjoy a meal while the rest of those servants in the room stood back and watched.

Even still, I didn't wish to be rude to my new employer, so I raised my fork and began to eat as delicately as I could.

"Lady Hayward tells me that you are the eldest of four sisters, Miss Honeyfield, is that correct?" Mr. Thorne said.

"Yes," I said.

"And that you play the pianoforte better than anyone she has ever heard?" he asked.

These pointed questions were making me flustered, even though I had answered them a dozen times already today. "My aunt is quite a flatterer," I said. "I am quite capable of playing, though I cannot imagine that I am truly the very best she has ever heard play."

"Modest, too, it seems," he said with a smile. "I think that is a trait that I would very much approve of my daughter learning."

"I will do my best, sir," I said.

As delicious as the food was, it was as if my stomach had disappeared entirely. I found I had no appetite and could only focus on Mr. Thorne and what he said.

"Did you find your room to be to your liking as well?" Mr. Thorne asked.

His gaze was quite sharp, and just from a brief exchange of eye contact, I could see great intelligence. He was a very well learned man, and yet he still demonstrated great kindness.

"I did, yes," I said. "Though I must admit that it will be quite strange not sharing a room with my sisters. I have done so ever since I was a young girl."

Mr. Thorne smiled. "I imagine that you must miss them terribly already, don't you?"

My eyes widened, and for a moment, I was quite caught off guard. To have such compassion for a young woman he had hired to help his daughter was baffling. I had heard much of the men in higher classes than I, and many stories had promised me self-superiority and condescension, not thoughtfulness and caring.

I dared not think too deeply about it, however. Perhaps he was simply trying to be kind so that I would work my very best.

"I do," I said. "But they are just a short ten miles from here. If something were to happen, I could walk there in a day, if I must."

"We will certainly never ask you to do that," Mr. Thorne said. He shifted his focus to his daughter, who was pushing some sugar peas around her plate with the end of her fork. "And what of you, my dear? What do you think of Miss Honeyfield coming to teach you how to play piano? It was very kind of her to do so, was it not?"

Miss Elizabeth turned her large eyes up to me,

but there was very little emotion there. Nothing more than a blank stare. "I suppose," she said in a flat tone.

"Oh, come now, dear," Mr. Thorne said, leaning over toward her. "You were very excited yesterday when I told you she was coming. You said you wanted her to teach you how to play all of the classics, and—"

He reached out to her to touch her hand, but she yanked it away with a sharp squeak.

Mr. Thorne's hand hovered over the table, precariously waiting. "Elizabeth, darling, I understand that today has been a long day and that there are some new changes to adjust to. But Miss Honeyfield came a long way in order to be your teacher, and I would like you to thank her."

Miss Elizabeth's gaze snapped up to mine, and once again, I was met with her unfeeling eyes. "You said she only traveled ten miles," she said. "We have traveled further than that to visit aunt and uncle."

Mr. Thorne's eyes narrowed. "My dear, you are quite missing the point."

Miss Elizabeth slammed her palm on the table, her silverware clattering across the table.

"Now, that is uncalled for, young lady," Mr. Thorne said, his voice growing deeper. "It is improper to show your frustrations at the dinner table in such a manner. Not only are you being very disrespectful, but you are dishonoring the newest member of our household."

"I do not care," said the girl, her bottom lip protruding. "I don't like her. I want her to go home."

It was as if I had been struck by a firm stick. How was it that just this afternoon she had sat down on the bench beside me and played a duet with me? And now she claims to have no affection for me?

"Elizabeth," Mr. Thorne said sternly. "You must apologize. I will not hear such talk in my house."

Miss Elizabeth pushed her chair back and vaulted from her seat, running from the room. Echoing cries followed after her.

"My apologies, Mr. Thorne. I shall fetch her," said Mr. Gibbs, who was standing near the door. He hurried from the room after her.

"I hope she's all right," I said, turning to look out into the hall. I could still hear her footsteps echoing off the polished floor as she ran.

"I must apologize, Miss Honeyfield," said Mr. Thorne. "I do wonder... How much did Miss Brown tell you about my daughter?"

Startled by the question, I turned to look at him.

"She said that she was somewhat immature for her age but that she was highly gifted."

"That is true," Mr. Thorne said, turning in his seat toward me. "However, the doctors believe that it might be something else entirely."

A prickle of fear washed over me. "What do you mean, exactly?"

"They can't quite explain it. She behaves rather normally for a young girl, most of the time. But it seems that when there is a great deal of change, or perhaps too much happening around her, she seems to revert to being a young girl once again. She simply cannot stand it. She runs around, kicking and screaming, almost as if there was too much happening inside that small head of hers…"

He stared out into the hall, and I saw genuine concern behind those blue-green eyes.

"The doctors think that she has weaknesses in some areas of her life but possesses great strength in others, almost as if she borrows her skills from ordinary behaviors and has somehow shifted them into another. For example, her ability to play the piano is superior to all her other skills, including most social abilities. She has a hard time empathizing with anyone, and no matter what I do, I cannot seem to help her understand the proper way to carry herself with others around. It can be quite frustrating," he said.

I could only imagine. "She seemed perfectly pleasant when I met her this afternoon," I said. "Perhaps a bit aloof, but most children are that way. It is quite easy to teach them how to behave, and yet they don't fully understand why until they are older."

"I suppose that's quite true," Mr. Thorne said. "And I expect you would know that, being the eldest of your siblings. I was the youngest, you see."

He scratched his cleanly shaven face, sighing.

"I do hope that giving her specific instruction time for her music will help her to overcome some of her weaknesses," he said. "The doctors said that by encouraging her strengths, it is possible that it would allow her to grow stronger and possibly move past herself. I am not certain if that is possible, but I am certainly willing to try."

He looked up at me, his gaze steady.

"I imagine I should have been more upfront with you about Elizabeth's behavior," he said in a quieter voice. "I hope you do not think I have brought you here under false pretenses."

"Not at all," I said. "She is quite the gifted child. We played together for some time, and I am rather impressed with her talent. She has great potential.

And music is nothing more than another form of discipline. It teaches one to be diligent and focused. It might be the very thing that she needs."

"It sounds as if you are up to the task, Miss Honeyfield?" Mr. Thorne asked.

"I am indeed," I said with a nod. "It will be my pleasure to help Miss Elizabeth."

"Wonderful," Mr. Thorne said. "You do not know how much joy that brings me. Thank you for your dedication. Elizabeth will become quite fond of you, I am certain of it."

The sound of the poor girl's tears echoed in my mind, but I held fast to the memory of us playing together that afternoon. "I believe we will become good friends," I said. "All it will take is a little time."

5

I slept far more peacefully than I imagined I would. I was so used to hearing the shifting and turning of my sisters in the middle of the night that I found the utter silence quite troubling as I lay my head down. The manor wasn't without its own noises, though, as servants tended to fires and brought clothes to the rooms of those who had not yet received them earlier in the day.

When I awoke the next morning, I was surprised to see the sunlight streaming in through the window.

Apparently, the silence wasn't quite as oppressive as I thought.

I threw open the window and let in the cool, dewy breeze of the morning. It carried in with it the fresh scent of honeysuckle blossoms and the comfort of warm grass.

I set about getting dressed, not lingering in the water closet for very long. I knew how incredibly fortunate I was to be able to have access to such a thing; back home, it wasn't until recently that we had anything of the sort. Father insisted, though, as Mother's health declined.

I meandered downstairs and into the kitchen to find something to eat before meeting Miss Brown and Miss Elizabeth at seven o'clock. There I met the cheery Mr. Able, who was the manor's cook, and his three servers and attendants.

"You're quite a welcome smile," Mr. Able said brightly as he tended to some potatoes, scrubbing them with a wire brush. "Everyone around here can be so glum all the time."

"I see no point in being glum, sir," I said. "There is far too much to be done to allow one's emotions to cloud their thoughts."

"Well said, my dear," said Mr. Able, grinning. I noticed a tooth missing along the bottom row, but he didn't seem to mind any. "Here, have some freshly baked bread," he said. "And make sure to bring some to Miss Brown. She never has breakfast, and I worry that the poor girl is going to shrivel up and die one day."

"Of course," I said. "And you wouldn't by any chance have an apple, would you?"

Mr. Able laughed. "An apple? Well, it just so happens I do. I'm making some apple pie for the master for dinner. I could spare one, perhaps. What did you need it for?"

"Encouragement," I said. "Do you know if Miss Elizabeth likes apples?"

"Indeed she does," Mr. Able said. "I think having an orchard behind the house has certainly helped with that. Let me fetch it for you." He turned and made his way into the larder, returning a moment later with a small, round, red fruit with a single streak of green through the flesh. "First apples of the season," he said. "Early this year, too."

"Wonderful," I said. "Thank you, Mr. Able."

"You're quite welcome, Miss," he said. "And don't forget your bread!"

I tucked the torn chunk of bread underneath my arm and held the apple tightly in my hand as I made my way back upstairs. I headed down the western hall, but soon found that I didn't recognize my surroundings.

I had been certain that all I needed to do was

take the first left, but it seemed that my memory had failed me.

"Miss Honeyfield."

A sharp voice made me turn around.

Mrs. Frampton stood at the end of the hall, a collection of parchment clutched in her hand.

"Mrs. Frampton," I said, curtseying. "I appear to be lost."

"Quite," she said, arching an eyebrow. "The school room is on the southern side of the house."

"Oh," I said. "Of course. My apologies."

"You may have impressed Mr. Thorne last night," she said to me as I passed by her in the hall. "But I have yet to see your worth. Do not disappoint me."

With those words, she turned on her heel and strode down the hall, her footsteps echoing off the wooden walls.

I hurried down the hall, trying not to draw too much attention to myself, and soon found a part of the hall that seemed more familiar than not. I heard voices, too, and as I stepped into the room, I realized I had finally found the right place.

"Ah, good morning, Miss Honeyfield," said Miss Brown from her chair at the table in the center of the room. "How wonderful it is to see you."

"Good morning," I said. I looked around the

room, and apart from a maid who was tidying up some of Miss Elizabeth's toys, it was only the two of us in the room. "Has Miss Elizabeth not come down yet?"

"She eats breakfast with her father until just before eight, where he brings her down here to me," she said, smiling up at me. "Ah, what is that you have in your arms?"

I withdrew the handkerchief with the bread and set it on the table. "From Mr. Able, for you and me. He said you hardly ever have breakfast, and he is concerned about you."

"That persistent old fool…" she said. Even still, she pulled the handkerchief toward herself and tore the piece of bread in half before pushing some of it toward me. "There you are. If I am to eat, then so are you."

And so we did. As we enjoyed the buttery, flaky bread, Miss Brown explained the schedule of her day with Miss Elizabeth. They started off with reading, followed by writing. In the afternoon, they would practice etiquette, as well as languages. Then they would alternate arithmetic and science every other day, so as to not overwhelm her.

"And then in the last hours of the day, I allow her to play with her music," she said. "I have found that it is a reward in her eyes, and it gives her a chance to focus on accomplishing what she needs so she can have fun at the end of it all."

"I think that's a marvelous idea," I said.

Miss Brown's eyes fell to the apple that I had set down in front of me. "What is the apple for?"

"Encouragement," I said. "For Miss Elizabeth."

"Very well," she said. "I look forward to whatever it is you are planning."

The door to the school room opened, and Miss Elizabeth stepped through with Mrs. Frampton.

"I'm pleased to see you found your way," she said in a rather dry voice.

"With your direction, how could I have done anything else?" I asked.

Her eyes narrowed. "Here you are, Miss Elizabeth," she said, giving the girl a nudge into the room. "Now you behave for Miss Brown. We do not need any more tantrums today. Am I clear?"

Miss Elizabeth nodded, her blonde curls bouncing.

"Very good," Mrs. Frampton said. "Off you go."

Mrs. Frampton closed the door to the school room, leaving the three of us alone.

"There we are," Miss Brown said. "Yes, come in, Miss Elizabeth. How was your breakfast?"

Miss Elizabeth's gaze moved to me as I slid the apple off the table, hiding it from her view. "It was very nice, thank you," she said, her face unchanging.

She slid into the chair beside my own and folded her hands in her lap.

"Now, today is going to be very exciting," Miss Brown said, a twinkle in her eyes. "Miss Honeyfield is going to sit in with us, and then this afternoon, she is going to play piano with you. How does that sound?"

Miss Elizabeth turned her eyes up to me, her expression blank. "Wonderful," she said in a flat tone.

I smiled down at her. "I look forward to it. Miss Brown tells me that it is your favorite time of day."

She nodded.

"Very good," I said. "And, if you are well behaved today, I have a surprise for you."

Her blue-green eyes widened at that. "A surprise?"

I nodded. "Indeed. But you must not mention it again, and you must be a very good listener to Miss Brown today."

Miss Brown smiled at me from across the table. I could see that she and I were going to be getting along just fine.

"Very good," Miss Brown said. "This morning, I thought we could begin by reading some fiction. Are you familiar with *Gulliver's Travels,* Miss Honeyfield?"

"Indeed I am," I said. "Reading was one of my favorite past time as a little girl. *Gulliver's Travels* was something my father read to me almost every night before I went to sleep. He rather liked the adventure, I think."

"You have a father, too?" Miss Elizabeth asked.

"Why, yes," I said with a small laugh. "And he is a very good man."

Miss Elizbeth nodded. "I see," she said.

I observed Miss Elizabeth's studies that day. It was fascinating to see just how brilliant she was and yet how little she seemed to disregard social graces. She had no problem at all completing a rather complex writing assignment but struggled to thank Miss Brown when she did as Miss Elizabeth asked.

We had lunch all together in the school room, which consisted of small sandwiches Mr. Able had made for us, along with some fresh spring onions and salted meats. Everything was delicious, and I found myself wishing that my sisters were with me so they, too, could enjoy these delectable creations.

Soon, though, it was time for her music lesson,

and I found myself rather nervous. It wasn't as if I had never taught someone else to play. It had just been many years since the necessity had arisen, and I hoped that I could be a valuable asset to this house.

"Are you ready, Miss Elizabeth?" I asked from the piano bench underneath the window.

Miss Elizabeth had slipped off to her dollhouse, which sat in the opposite corner. She seemed intent on her dolls, brushing their hair and fluffing their dresses. It was sweet to see, but Miss Brown had told her she could have a quarter of an hour to play, which had come and gone.

Miss Brown was seated at the writing desk near the fireplace, correcting some of Miss Elizabeth's arithmetic questions. She turned to see Miss Elizabeth still seated in front of her doll house. "Miss Elizabeth, I believe Miss Honeyfield was speaking to you."

Miss Elizabeth, however, seemed to have gone momentarily deaf.

Miss Brown looked over at me and shook her head. "Sometimes she does this," she said, rising from her seat.

I held up a hand to stop her. "One moment," I said. "Perhaps we can find a way to get her to listen."

I turned around in my seat, and set the shiny,

red apple on the corner of the piano, in plain sight for Miss Elizabeth. At the same time, I began to play a simple song, something soothing and lulling. I assumed it would make Miss Elizabeth relax and was certain it was something she was familiar with.

It wasn't long before I heard little footsteps making their way over to where I sat, my fingers gliding across the keys.

"Miss Honeyfield, why do you have an apple?" she asked, pointing to the succulent fruit on the piano.

"For encouragement," I said, just as I had before.

She tilted her head. "Encouragement for what?" she asked.

"For you," I said. I slid over on the bench and pat the pink, silken fabric. "Come join me, and I'll show you."

Miss Elizabeth happily hopped up onto the bench, peering up at me.

"Now," I said, lifting the apple. "We are going to play a game."

"A game?" Miss Elizabeth asked.

I nodded. "Indeed. A game that I used to play with my sisters when they were very small. Would you like to learn it?"

"Yes, please," Miss Elizabeth said, her eyes on the apple.

I rose from the stool and made my way to the table. There I had tucked a knife into the other handkerchief I had brought up to the school room with me.

I carried it back over to the piano and began to slice up the apple into luscious slices.

"Here is the game," I said, setting each slice onto the clean handkerchief. "Every time you play a song correctly, or you follow my instructions without trouble, you will receive a slice of the apple. You win the game if you are able to collect all eight slices."

"Do I get to eat them if I get them?" Miss Elizabeth asked.

"But of course," I said. "That is what makes the game so fun."

We were about three songs in, and already I had parted with five of my apple slices. When she put her mind to something, Miss Elizabeth truly was an angelic child.

Just as she finished a fourth song, an applause reached us from the other side of the room. She and I both turned on the bench and saw Mr. Thorne standing there with Miss Brown, watching.

"Father, did you hear?" Miss Elizabeth said excitedly, sliding down off the bench and hurrying over to him. "Did you see how well I played?"

"Indeed I did," he said, laying a hand on her shoulder. "And it seems that Miss Honeyfield has found one of your favorite treats, hasn't she?"

Miss Elizabeth nodded as she bit down on another slice of apple.

He looked over her head and grinned at me. He really was a kind-faced man. "Thank you very much, Miss Honeyfield. I came in to see how your first day was going, and it seems that I worried for nothing. Your experience with your many sisters certainly has paid off, has it not?"

"It certainly has taught me patience," I said. "Miss Elizabeth was the image of studious today. She was focused and attentive."

"I am pleased to hear it," he said. "And I am also quite pleased that you are as talented as you are. I have no talent for music myself."

"But you have such a great appreciation for it, sir," Miss Brown said.

"I did not always," he said, his smile faltering. "My wife was the one who truly loved it. It seems that her gifts have been passed on to our daughter."

My heart sank for him. I had wondered where Mrs. Thorne might have been...

Miss Elizabeth, who had been wearing a smile just a moment before, suddenly became quite upset. "Mother... Mother loved the piano," she said.

Then she dissolved into tears, running over to Miss Brown and throwing her arms around her waist.

Mr. Thorne's face paled, and he watched her go with dismay. It was clear he regretted saying anything in the first place. "I should know better by now not to say anything quite so flippantly to her," he said, straightening his coat uncomfortably. "My apologies, Miss Honeyfield. I should have more sense than that."

"No, it's quite all right," I said.

"She has been so fragile since her mother's passing last year," he said. "As have I, to be honest. But I cannot help but wonder if some of her struggles are not because of losing her mother."

"It is quite possible," I said. "As sad as that is to say. And I understand perfectly what that's like."

"What?" Mr. Thorne asked, glancing over at me.

"Losing a mother," I said rather simply.

My eyes were fixed on the poor girl who was crying against Miss Brown. Miss Brown was doing what she could to console her, but it was no use, it seemed.

I could feel Mr. Thorne's gaze on my face, yet he did not any further questions, which surprised me. I was appreciative of the respect he showed me.

Even still... In that moment, I felt something, as if Mr. Thorne and I understood one another a little better than we had before.

6

The warm days of July gave way to the long days of August, where the peak of summer came and went. Every day that I awoke at Northington Park, the more I felt like I belonged there. I found time to enjoy the lovely scenery; I wandered in the gardens, picked flowers with Miss Elizabeth, and sat beneath the boughs of the apple trees in the orchard.

I learned a great many things about those that lived in Northington Park. Miss Brown, for instance, was a widow. She and her husband had been married six short years before he was killed in the war. Knowing she was likely far too old to marry again, she decided to take on the role of governess and had been serving Mr. Thorne and Miss Elizabeth for nearly five years now.

Mr. Able was quite the charitable sort of man, even when the others around him weren't quite the same. He was always more than happy to have a chat and more often than not would allow me to sample whatever it was he was preparing for that night's supper. I had yet to try something of his that was not excellent.

Mr. Thorne was still somewhat of a mystery to me. As much as I had seen him my first week at Northington Park, he had been far scarcer since. Miss Brown said that he was very busy, and many afternoons he was away from the manor making social calls. When we did have a chance to speak, however, he was kind and polite. But I realized that we only ever discussed his daughter. I knew nothing of him personally, save that he himself was a widower and had little musical talent. I found myself curious to know more, especially since he was my employer, and I wished to understand him, and his daughter, a bit better.

Regardless, I was finding that I was very pleased here at Northington Park.

It was a bright August morning when I sat down at my desk to write a letter to my sisters. Mr. Thorne had taken Miss Elizabeth down to town for the morning, and I found myself wanting to keep my sisters informed about what was happening.

I broke the seal on the new ink pot. I had used up the rest of what I had brought answering a letter from Aunt Patience the week before. She had asked so many questions that it had taken me three whole pieces of parchment to reply. I was grateful that Miss Brown had given me permission to take whatever I needed from the school room.

Dear Amelia, Isabella, and Susannah, I wrote.

It is hard to believe that I have been at Northington Park for six weeks already. They have certainly passed quickly, as I have had a great deal of new responsibilities to undertake. My days are becoming more familiar, and even though they are quite different from what I am used to, I must admit that I am rather enjoying the tasks I have been given.

My mornings are rather simple. I wake and have some quiet, alone time in my room where I read and perhaps write some. Then I enjoy a breakfast with Miss Brown in the kitchens. Miss Brown is the governess here at Northington Park, and she and I have quite taken a liking to one another. It is almost as if she were an elder sister, though I imagine you three would be able to attest to that fact.

Then we spend most of the day with Miss Elizabeth, our charge and student. She is quite the remarkable young girl. She is very gifted with music, almost as if she does it without thinking. She does, however, struggle in other areas, as all children do.

We have begun to understand one another, Miss Elizabeth and I. For instance, I have learned that she positively loves apples. She is also rather fond of kittens. I have told her that I quite like sweet rolls and am a bit bossy at times. We are becoming friends, albeit it slowly.

I looked up from my letter and tapped my fingers against the table. I knew that I could spend several hours compiling a letter with everything I wished to say, yet also knew that would not be the best use of my time. I did have a great deal to take care of that day, and my sisters would surely be busy as well.

It was best to keep it to the important matters.

I think I am settling in here very well. Please ensure to tell Father that I love him dearly and pray for him often. I do hope that things have been better for him, and for the rest of you, in these last weeks. The pain of losing Mother will likely never fully leave us, but perhaps, with time, it will grow easier to bear.

All my love,

Juliana

I signed the letter and read it over, ensuring I had

not missed anything I wished to say. Satisfied, I sealed it with the Thorne family crest and rose from my seat to carry it down to Mr. Gibbs, who would hopefully be able to mail it today.

I spent my lunch time once again with Miss Brown. We talked literature and poetry, and other topics that I found invigorating.

"I am quite pleased to have someone to discuss these topics with," I said as I spread a layer of soft cheese on the piece of bread I had acquired. "My sisters found it dull to speak of such things for great lengths of time."

"Indeed," she said. "My sisters, too, seemed more interested in fashion and art than they were about anything else. I love them dearly, but sometimes I wish for something more, yes?"

I smiled at her as I poured some milk into my tea.

A knock at the door drew our attention. "Come in," Miss Brown said, rising to her feet.

I, too, followed her and stood as well.

The door swung inward, and Mr. Thorne stepped in with Miss Elizabeth. Upon one look at her face, I could see that she was rather displeased about something.

"Good afternoon, ladies," Mr. Thorne said.

"Good afternoon," Miss Brown and I said, curtseying.

"I apologize for our tardiness, but Miss Elizabeth was having a great deal of amusement in town," Mr. Thorne said. "However, amusement turned quickly into trouble when she did not wish to accompany me home." He gave Miss Elizabeth a sharp look.

Miss Elizabeth folded her arms and looked away, her chin pointed into the air.

He shook his head. "Mr. Garver had brought his ponies into town, and Miss Elizabeth wished to pet them. Then, Mr. Garver gave her some sugar cubes to share with them. She was delighted and wished to give them more. Mr. Garver said that the sugar was a special treat the ponies only received on occasion, but Miss Elizabeth was rather unhappy with his response. Weren't you, Miss Elizabeth?"

Miss Elizabeth let out a rather loud "Hmph!"

Mr. Thorne looked back at Miss Brown and me. "To be quite honest, I am beside myself with her today. I apologize that I have brought her home in such a state. I fear that she may be less than agreeable during her lessons this afternoon."

"Never you worry, Mr. Thorne," Miss Brown said, hurrying over to Miss Elizabeth. "We will find a way to settle her down. Everything will be just fine."

He nodded, his hands folded behind his back. "Very well," he said. "I leave her in your capable hands, then. I must go speak with Mr. Gibbs about some letters I received today."

He turned and left the school room.

"Father, no!" Miss Elizabeth said, throwing herself in the direction of her father's departing back. "Please, do not leave me in here."

"Now, Miss Elizabeth," said Miss Brown, kneeling down in front of her. "It's quite all right. I know that today is a bit strange, but we can still have a perfectly ordinary afternoon. What do you think?"

Miss Elizabeth's bottom lip protruded and she dipped her head. "I want my father."

"I understand that," Miss Brown said. "But we must focus on our work for a little while today. Just like your father must take care of things, so should you. Can you act grown up like your father for a little while?"

Miss Elizabeth lifted her head, nodding glumly.

"There's a good girl," Miss Brown said, guiding her over to the school table.

Miss Brown gave me a rather exasperated look, shaking her head.

I admired her persistence. It was clear that she knew Elizabeth rather well and was able to find just the right thing to say in order to motivate her. It seemed that I still had a great deal to learn about her.

I found myself a seat at the far end of the table to wait for Miss Elizabeth's lesson time. As I watched her and Miss Brown, though, it became quite clear that she was having a much more difficult time concentrating than usual. It was frustrating Miss Brown a great deal, and more than once I heard her use a rather sharp tone with the girl, who then would frown more deeply in reply.

Soon, though, it was time for her music lessons, and I breathed a sigh of great relief. Surely, she would be excited to sit down and play at her piano for some time, right?

I had no idea what to expect, though.

"All right, Miss Elizabeth, you may have one moment to stretch your legs before you go sit down for your piano lesson," Miss Brown said. "I know how much you are looking forward to it, but you have been sitting so long, and—"

She looked up at the same time I did, and we both caught Miss Elizabeth staring at me with wide, round eyes.

"What is it, Miss Elizabeth?" I asked. "Are you all right?"

She didn't appear to hear me. Her gaze was vacant, and there were dark circles under her eyes. Was she perhaps simply exhausted?

"Come along, Miss Elizabeth," Miss Brown said, walking around the table toward her. "Let us begin your lesson. Your father will not be pleased if we are late to dinner once again."

"No!" Miss Elizabeth shouted, and she took off across the room to the door. She grabbed onto the door handle and pulled it open, running out into the hall and beyond.

"Miss Elizabeth!" Miss Brown said, her jaw falling open. "In all my time, I have never…" She did not finish her sentence as she took off through the hall after her.

My heart leapt into my throat, and worry stripped me of any exhaustion I felt. I looked about the room, but there was nothing I could do here. I decided it was best if I went after her, as well.

I heard Miss Elizabeth shriek from further down the hall, nearer the main staircase. I hurried off after them, passing by a young maid who had stopped to stare, her eyes widened.

"Is she all right?" the maid asked.

"She will be," I said and continued down the hall.

I could see Miss Elizabeth's blonde curls at the far end of the eastern wing. Miss Brown was doing her best to keep up, her skirts lifted so as to not trip on the hem.

"Miss Elizabeth, please," Miss Brown said. "You are making quite the commotion right now."

"Father!" Miss Elizabeth cried. "Father, please! Where are you?"

She stopped at a crossroads and hurried down the left hall, Miss Brown not far behind.

I had not yet been to this part of the manor and was greeted with another long hall lined with portraits and candelabras. Miss Elizabeth was nearly at the far end, banging against a door with her tiny fists.

"Father!" she yelled.

"Miss Elizabeth, please," Miss Brown said. "You don't need to—"

"What is going on here?" came a voice through the door that Miss Elizabeth was banging on.

I came to a stop nearby.

Miss Brown laid her hands on Miss Elizabeth's shoulders, but Miss Elizabeth thrashed and shoved her hands away. "No!" Miss Elizabeth yelled.

The door swung inward, and Mr. Thorne stepped out.

"Elizabeth, dear, what is the matter?" he asked, looking down at her. "What has you so agitated?"

She threw her arms around his waist and began to sob. "I don't want to. I don't want to!" she said.

"You don't want to do what, dear?" Mr. Thorne said.

I glanced over his shoulder and saw a room behind Mr. Thorne. It was not a room that I had seen before. Mr. Thorne's study was beside the library, yet the room beyond seemed to be something akin to an office of some sort. Books were stacked on shelves along the back wall, but there were also trinkets that I could not quite make out from that distance. Along the closer wall, a sword hung on a plaque, sheathed, yet it looked quite old. I thought I had also caught a glimpse of an old military jacket of some sort hanging on a peg.

"I am terribly sorry, Mr. Thorne," Miss Brown said. "I do not know what has come over the poor girl. She is inconsolable. She ran from the school room as if something terrible had happened."

I felt a gaze on me, and I shifted my eyes.

Mr. Thorne was watching me, his eyes narrowing.

Reaching behind himself, he took the doorknob in his hand and pulled the door shut.

A small twinge of worry passed down my spine. There was some sort of hardness in his gaze that I was unaccustomed to.

"It's all right, Elizabeth," Mr. Thorne said, wrapping his arm around her and leading her away from the door. "Perhaps it would be best if we cancel lessons for the rest of the day. I imagine anything we try now simply will not be productive."

"Of course, Mr. Thorne," Miss Brown said, bowing her head.

I followed suit, dipping my gaze.

He and Miss Elizabeth walked past us, and Miss Brown did not straighten until they were at the other end of the hall.

"Well…" Miss Brown said, brushing her hands across her skirt. "I do hope that Miss Elizabeth will be all right."

"Indeed," I said, my gaze on Mr. Thorne's back as they made their way around the corner. "Though I wonder what that was all about?"

7

Miss Brown and I returned to the school room where we cleaned up from the lessons yet hardly spoke to one another. I noticed the furrowed brow on her face as she tucked books away back onto the shelf and picked up Miss Elizabeth's dolls and set them back inside the dollhouse. Her nervousness was setting me on edge, as well.

I hoped more than anything that we had not upset Mr. Thorne.

As I arranged some sheet music for the next day's lesson, I could not help but think about what I had seen in that hallway. Miss Elizabeth's behavior was distressing, for certain. But that was not my primary concern.

What my mind kept drifting toward was the look on Mr. Thorne's face when I had seen the inside of that room.

I had never been told there were rooms in the house that were off limits, yet there were many places that I simply did not enter. For one, I had never seen Mr. Thorne's room, and I had only entered Miss Elizabeth's once when she wished to show me the piano that her father had placed in her room.

Yet, it seemed that the room Mr. Thorne had so clearly closed to us this afternoon was one he truly did not wish for us to see.

What did he keep in there?

I realized that I was nothing more than a tutor and that I had no right to the man's business, but something troubled me in his gaze. It was not the look of an employer keeping distance from his daughter's tutor. It was more like a look a guilty man wore in order to keep secrets.

That was a troubling thought. I knew that I hardly knew Mr. Thorne, but what I had seen of him, I rather liked. He had been kind to me since taking me in, and I appreciated his affections for his daughter.

Why did this unsettle me so?

Over the next few days, Miss Brown and Miss Elizabeth acted as if nothing had happened. After some rest and a break, it seemed that Miss Elizabeth was back to her usual self. She smiled at me as she crawled up onto the piano bench the next day, and I took it in stride.

"Did your mother play the piano with you?" Miss Elizabeth asked as we wrapped up the song we had been practicing.

"She did," I said. "She loved the piano, just like your mother did."

Miss Elizabeth nodded. "My mother liked to do a lot of things with me. I miss them."

"Well, what sort of things did she do?" I asked.

Miss Elizabeth shrugged.

"Did she play with your dolls with you?" I asked.

She nodded.

"What of reading to you?" I asked.

"Yes, she did that, too," Miss Elizabeth said.

She then went on to tell me about other ways her mother took care of her, things that her father would likely have never known, such as adjusting the ribbons on her dress just so, as well as practicing her French with her. They would spend afternoons in the kitchens learning to bake, and apparently, they shared a very special tea together on rare occasions.

After her lessons, I pulled Miss Brown aside. "If it is agreeable to you, I would like to take on more responsibilities for Miss Elizabeth," I said.

"Well, certainly," Miss Brown said. "But why do you ask so suddenly?"

I glanced over my shoulder to ensure that no one was there. "It seems to me that in her mother's absence, Miss Elizabeth has missed certain activities they used to do together. I am well aware that I could never take her mother's place, but perhaps I could help you by doing some of these simpler tasks for her, things that might make her feel more at peace. I am certain that neither of us would like to see her as frustrated as she was the other day."

"Indeed," Miss Brown said. "I think it is a fine idea. What did you have in mind?"

The more I considered it, the more I wondered if Mr. Thorne's harsh stare was not as a result of a father's anger in response to his daughter's unrest. Perhaps I had misread his reaction entirely. And the best way to ensure that I kept my job, and therefore Mr. Thorne happy, was to keep Miss Elizabeth calm.

That was the beginning of my greater responsibilities around Northington Park.

August moved smoothly into September, and the arid days became began to give way to cooler, wetter ones. I was more familiar with my surroundings and even found I rather liked living in Northington Park. I was amazed that I had been able to survive at home as long as I had with all of us living in such a small space as our cottage.

Letters from home were encouraging, as well. It seemed that Aunt Patience was keeping her word and watching after Father and my sisters. According to Amelia, it seemed she was taking complete credit for my newly acquired status. I paid it no mind. If it wasn't for her, I never would have been as fortunate as I was.

Miss Elizabeth also seemed to be taking to the new things I was doing for her, especially a new nightly ritual we had adopted. One night, I let it slip to her as we read together in the drawing room that my mother used to make me a special tea on nights when I struggled to fall asleep. Miss Elizabeth was reminded at once of the tea her own mother would make her and insisted that I make some for her.

Wishing to keep the peace, for my sake as well as hers, I agreed, though I wasn't entirely upset to find a way to bond with the young girl.

It was a rainy September night when I made my way down to the kitchens to make some tea for Miss

Elizabeth. It was dark and cool, and as I carried a candle, thunder shook the house.

I suppressed a shiver. Thunder always frightened me, even when I was a girl.

The kitchen was bustling as it always was. Mr. Able was busy preparing the next morning's breakfast. His two attendants were mixing dough and organizing vegetables for dinner the following evening.

There were other servants down there, as well, having their evening meal after all their other tasks were complete.

"Good evening, Miss Honeyfield," Mr. Able said with a wide grin. "Anything I can get for you?"

"Some tea, please, for two," I said. "I promised Miss Elizabeth I would make her the special tea my mother used to make."

"Oh, how wonderful," Mr. Able said. "What might you need?"

"Do you perhaps have Earl Grey leaves?" I asked. "And cream, instead of milk."

"Quite rich," Mr. Able said.

"It's quite soothing before sleep," I said. "And I shall warm the cream before taking it to her."

"My, she is certainly in for a treat," Mr. Able said. "I shall go fetch the tea leaves. Feel free to take the sugar you need from the ceramic over there." He pointed to the small crock on the shelf beside the sack of barley.

"Thank you," I said.

Mr. Able nodded and made his way out of the kitchen toward the larder.

I set about finding a proper tray to carry the tea up on. I filled a kettle with some water and hung it over the roaring fire in the hearth and went to the crate where Mr. Able kept the nicest silverware to find a proper spoon.

My back was turned to the other servants in the room, and I soon heard whispers from them as they thought I was not paying attention to them.

"...stopped outside, I could have sworn I heard something," said the maid with dark hair. I believe her name was Miss Sarah. "I'm not quite sure what, but he certainly seemed upset."

"We're coming up on it, you know," said the footman with cropped blonde hair. "The anniversary of his death."

My body stiffened. Death? Who were they talking about?

"Perhaps that was all it was," said Miss Sarah. "But even still, every time I walk past that place, it gives me great discomfort."

"He hasn't ever seen you nearby, has he?" the footman asked.

"No," Miss Sarah said. "But as I take clothes to his and Miss Elizabeth's rooms, it is quite difficult for me to not walk past it frequently."

I very nearly dropped the top of the sugar crock. She couldn't mean the room that I had seen Mr. Thorne coming out of, could she?

"It is best if you simply keep your distance," the footman said. "I truly see no reason to put yourself in harm's way."

It was too much for me to take. I turned around and stared at them, and both of them seemed caught off guard by my attention.

"My apologies," I said. "But are you referring to Mr. Thorne's private study?"

"Is that what that room is?" Miss Sarah asked, her eyes widening. "You have seen the inside of it?"

"Well, no," I said. "I caught a glimpse as Mr. Thorne was coming out of it a few weeks ago."

The footman and the maid exchanged a nervous look.

"What is it?" I asked. "What did you mean when you said avoiding it would ensure she would stay out of harm's way?"

"You have been here for months now and you

haven't heard about Mr. Thorne?" the footman asked.

A chill crept up my back. "Haven't heard what?" I asked.

"What is your opinion of the master of the house?" Miss Sarah asked, raising an eyebrow.

I glanced between them both. "I... I find Mr. Thorne to be very kind," I said. "He has been nothing but caring since I moved in here to help take care of Miss Elizabeth."

The footman nodded.

"What do you think of him?" I asked, my eyes narrowing.

The footman leaned forward, dropping his voice even further. "Mr. Thorne's brother, the one who was meant to inherit this estate in the first place, died in this very house."

I narrowed my gaze. "And what are you implying?"

They both exchanged wide-eyed looks, neither of them wishing to admit their thoughts out loud.

"Mr. Thorne inherited the fortune instead," said Sarah.

It took me a moment, but the realization of what they were implying began to settle on me.

It was as if I had been cloaked in ice. All the heat

was sapped from me, and all the strength left my limbs. I grabbed onto the table in front of me, desperate for the support. "You think Mr. Thorne was the one who—?" I asked. "I cannot imagine Mr. Thorne being capable of something like that."

"That's certainly what he wants you to believe," Miss Sarah said. "He is quite good at putting on airs in order to keep everyone at a distance. Haven't you thought him to be quite secretive? My cousin works for a Lord to the south, and he is very amiable. All of his staff trust him implicitly."

"Yes, and I was meant to work for Mr. Thorne's brother when he was to inherit Northington Park," the footman said. "But that was all before his death."

My throat became tight as I looked between them. "What proof have you?" I asked. "Do you really hold fast to rumors so easily?"

"You have not been here as long as we have," Miss Sarah said, folding her arms. "That room of his... I am not certain what he keeps, but it is nothing he wishes for anyone to see. Not even his own daughter."

"He won't allow Miss Elizabeth inside?" I asked.

"Certainly not," the footman said. "And she knows it quite well."

It made me wonder if Miss Elizabeth's tantrum

some weeks ago was not an attempt to enter that room she knew she had been barred from.

"My apologies, I am just having a difficult time believing this," I said.

"It's quite simple, really," said Miss Sarah. "Mr. Thorne stood to inherit a small fortune from his father, yet his brother was to inherit all of Northington Park. Have you no concept of greed or jealousy?"

"I certainly do," I said. "Yet I have never seen any sort of behavior in Mr. Thorne to indicate that he harbored anything in him like that."

"Neither have I," the footman said. "Which I believe is his way of atoning for his crime."

"If this was true, then why had no one come to investigate?" I asked. "Would his fortune have been bequeathed to another if he had been discovered guilty?"

"Perhaps," said Sarah. "But his alternative had been to enter the military, and something tells me that that sort of life would not have suited him."

"Yes, who wouldn't want to be the one who would inherit such a home and fortune when that was the sort of life to look forward to?" the footman said.

"That is the highest form of greed," I said,

shaking my head. "No. I cannot believe it. Mr. Thorne is a good man who loves his daughter. He would not be able to have those feelings if he had been able to... take someone else's life," I said.

The door into the kitchens opened, and Mr. Able strolled back in. "Here you are, Miss Honeyfield," he said with a broad smile. "The tea leaves you were looking for?"

"Yes, thank you," I said, ducking my eyes.

"Is everything quite all right in here?" Mr. Able asked. "It seems I walked into a rather tense moment."

"Everything is perfectly fine," I said, lifting the boiling kettle out of the hearth and setting it on the tray alongside the cream and sugar I had collected. "Perfectly fine indeed."

I lifted the tray and made my way from the room, the color high in my cheeks.

The impertinence of those two, talking so flippantly about Mr. Thorne. And in such a terrible manner, too.

I sagged against the wall out in the empty hall, attempting to catch my breath.

Mr. Thorne... Was it possible he truly was capable of something so horrific? I hardly knew him, and that made it easier to consider even believing what they said in the first place. They had worked here for some time, after all. How could I be certain they weren't mistaken?

That was the difficult thing about the truth sometimes. It didn't matter if you wanted it to be true or not. It was the truth, no matter how uncomfortable it might be.

I determined that I would not allow it to color my view of Mr. Thorne, or his daughter, by default. If anything, I needed to maintain appearances so that he did not become suspicious of me.

I set off back down the hall, tea in hand.

But even as I walked, I realized how easy it was to wonder whether or not something like that could possibly have happened.

8

The rainy weather seemed to be drawn to Northington Park for the first weeks of September. Every morning when I awoke, the droplets streaked down the window, and thunder rumbled overhead. Every afternoon, the school room was moody and dark, requiring Miss Brown and I to light candles earlier in the day so Miss Elizabeth could see to finish her studies. The fountains out behind the estate and the pond out front all flooded, the water levels rising every passing day, drenching the grass and pathways around it.

It was the middle of the month when the sun finally decided to show itself. It was bright and warm, and it seemed everyone attempted to find an excuse to be able to stand outside, even for just a moment, so they could feel the light upon their face.

Miss Brown, however, was less than inclined to step outside, let alone out of the school room.

"I am quite all right," she insisted as she covered her mouth once again, a barking cough escaping her. "All this rain has made it more difficult to get fresh air, and my room has been a bit drafty at night, and—" She stifled a sneeze.

"Miss Brown, you are ill," I said. "You must sit down before you make yourself worse."

"As I said, I am fine," she said, pulling some books off the shelf. "Now, when Miss Elizabeth arrives, we can begin."

Miss Elizabeth and Mr. Thorne arrived a short time later.

I found my eyes drawn to Mr. Thorne as he entered the room. Where I had once been quite pleased to see him, I felt a small shiver of fright at his presence.

"Good morning, Miss Honeyfield," he said as he saw me, a kind smile stretching across his face.

I dipped into a curtsey. "Good morning, sir," I said.

I didn't raise my eyes as he and Miss Elizabeth walked into the room.

"Good heavens, Miss Brown," Mr. Thorne said. "Your face is flushed. Are you well?"

"Of course," Miss Brown said rather indignantly. "I have never been—" But her words were cut off as she sneezed once more.

"Oh, dear," Mr. Thorne said, taking a step closer to Miss Brown. "Do you have a fever?"

"I..." she said, sniffling. "I do not think so."

I walked across the room, and against her protests, laid my palm to her forehead.

"She does," I said, taking a step back.

"Well, there is no helping it, then," Mr. Thorne said. "Miss Brown, you are to spend the rest of the day in bed. I shall send some soup and tea up to your room, but you are to focus on getting well again."

"But Miss Elizabeth's lessons," Miss Brown said. "Her routine."

"She will be fine for a day or two," Mr. Thorne said. "Won't you, Elizabeth?"

Miss Elizabeth's eyes were focused on Miss Brown. "Are you going to be well, Miss Brown?" she asked.

"Of course, dear," Miss Brown said, kneeling

before Miss Elizabeth. "I am quite all right. I do not even think I need to—"

"Miss Brown," Mr. Thorne said with a hint of amusement.

"Yes," Miss Brown said, rising to her feet. She looked over at me. "I suppose I shall leave her lessons to you for the day," she said. "If that's all right with you?"

"Oh," I said, my cheeks coloring. "I suppose I could…"

"Very well," Miss Brown said. "But not a day more than I need." She turned and headed toward the door, stopping just as she was to step outside. "And thank you, Mr. Thorne, for your kindness."

"You are quite welcome," Mr. Thorne said.

As Miss Brown headed down the hall, we heard her sneeze, as well as moan with relief.

"Well," Mr. Thorne said, turning to Miss Elizabeth and me. "I know that we should keep up with your lessons, my dear, but the weather is far too nice to pass up today. What say you to a walk in the gardens?"

"Oh, yes please, Father," Miss Elizabeth said, nearly jumping on the balls of her feet, her skirts bouncing. "I would so very much like to be outside."

"It is settled then," he said, looking up at me.

"And of course you will join us, right, Miss Honeyfield?"

My eyes widened as I stared at him. "Oh, you wish for me to join?" I asked.

"Oh, please, Miss Honeyfield," she said, grabbing onto my hands and squeezing them. "It is such a lovely day. We mustn't miss it."

"Are you sure?" I asked. "You do not wish to spend the time with your father?"

"We can all be together," Miss Elizabeth said.

I supposed I had no choice but to agree.

The weather truly was lovely as we stepped outside, and at once I was glad I had gone with them. It felt wonderful to stretch my legs. I could not remember the last time I was out of doors.

Miss Elizabeth was all too pleased to have a chance to run and play. Miss Brown always encouraged her to act like the young lady she was, even when she was outside, but I appreciated that she still recognized that Miss Elizabeth was a child and certainly needed time to allow her imagination to take over.

She ran along the path ahead of Mr. Thorne and me, leaving the two of us walking side by side in the morning sunlight.

As much as I had attempted to convince myself

that the rumors about Mr. Thorne's brother were not true, it was incredibly difficult to truly believe that now that he was standing beside me, walking along with me as if nothing had changed.

To him, nothing had changed, but it certainly made me wonder if he had heard the rumors that everyone was spreading about him.

"Miss Honeyfield," Mr. Thorne said, startling me.

"Yes?" I asked, perhaps a bit too quickly.

"Do you believe that Miss Elizabeth's lessons are progressing?" he asked, his hands clasped behind his back.

"Oh, yes," I said. "Indeed, I do, sir. She has been doing very well. Every day when she comes to sit at the bench, she seems eager to learn and has been quite attentive."

"That's very good," Mr. Thorne said. "And her behavior?"

"She has been the image of perfection," I said. "Courteous, respectful, and even quite encouraging. She is frustrated when she makes mistakes, but it has been quite amazing to see that she then strives to correct those errors and always wishes to improve herself. It's quite impressive."

"That is wonderful news," Mr. Thorne said. "I'm

glad to hear that she has been maturing under the tutelage of you and Miss Brown."

"Oh, I cannot claim to have done very much, Mr. Thorne," I said. "Miss Brown truly is the one who has given Miss Elizabeth all she has learned."

"Yes, but do you know the name I hear most often at night when she and I are seated in the drawing room together?" Mr. Thorne asks, a twinkle in his eye.

My eyes widened.

"Yours," Mr. Thorne said. "It has been quite a long time since I have seen her quite as excited about something in such a long time."

We came around a rather large tree with low hanging boughs. The shade was lovely, despite the fact that I was relishing the sunshine.

Mr. Thorne's footsteps slowed to a stop, and I stopped as well.

Miss Elizabeth was standing before a carved stone statue in the middle of a beautiful garden that I had never seen before. The hedges surrounding it were perfectly manicured, and a large stone fountain was situated behind it, bubbling merrily in the sunlight.

I stared at the statue and realized it was the likeness of a woman. Or maybe, perhaps an angel. She stood in a very elegant, subdued manner, her eyes looking upward toward the heavens.

Miss Elizabeth was looking up at the statue, her arms hanging at her sides.

"I suppose I should have expected she would run here," Mr. Thorne said in a subdued voice.

It was a quiet sort of place where one might come to walk and enjoy some peace. I would imagine sitting on the stone bench along the hedgerows with a book in hand, whiling away the afternoon.

"It is quite lovely," I said.

"Lovely, perhaps," Mr. Thorne said. "Yet a place of great sorrow, as well."

I looked more closely at Miss Elizabeth, who was staring up at the statue. Her small frame was perfectly still, and I understood what Mr. Thorne meant. Miss Elizabeth's joy could not be contained when she felt it; she would move and dance and sing.

To look at her now, though, it was as if she were experiencing some deep, long endured pain that I could only attempt to understand.

The statue, the garden, the overall feeling of reverence...

My heart fluttered.

"Is this, perhaps... where Mrs. Thorne was laid to rest?" I asked.

Silence greeted my question, and the only sounds I heard were the wind through the trees and the trickle of the fountain's water.

"Yes," said Mr. Thorne. "Before she passed, she requested to be buried here, at Northington Park. This was her home, her greatest joy."

I turned to look at him, and I was startled by the hurt I saw so plain in his eyes.

"She said she wished to remain close to Elizabeth and me, so that we would always remember her love for us," he said.

Miss Elizabeth's face turned back toward us, her eyes wide yet not stained with tears like I had expected.

"I am ashamed to admit that it has been some time since we have come to pay our respects," he said and began to walk slowly toward the statue.

I was uncertain about whether or not I should follow after. It was a rather intimate moment between father and daughter that I felt I might be intruding upon.

For several moments, I stood alongside the tree with the low-hanging boughs, the wind rustling through the leaves, watching Mr. Thorne and Miss Elizabeth.

Mr. Thorne laid his hand on Miss Elizabeth's shoulder, and they stood together at the foot of the statue, as if having a moment as a family that had been long overdue.

"Miss Honeyfield!"

I looked down, hearing Miss Elizabeth's voice calling out to me.

She waved me down toward them.

I hesitated, and it wasn't until I saw Mr. Thorne turn and smile at me that I knew it was fine.

"This is my mother, Miss Honeyfield," Miss Elizabeth said, pointing up at the poised carved woman in the stone. "She looks just like I remember."

"She was very lovely," I said.

She peered up at me. "Father says that no one would ever replace Mother, but he did say that one day I may have another woman who could take care of me like Mother would have."

"I think that would be wonderful," I said.

"Perhaps she will even love music like you do," Miss Elizabeth said. "Or maybe she will share tea with me like you do, Miss Honeyfield. And I hope that she will smile at me and be patient with me like you are, Miss Honeyfield."

I looked down at her, and my heart swelled with affection for the young girl. I smiled down at her. "Whoever she may be, I know that she will love you unconditionally."

Miss Elizabeth seemed quite pleased by this, swinging on her father's arm. "Father, let us continue on our walk. Mother always loved walks."

"Indeed she did," Mr. Thorne said.

Miss Elizabeth began to hum and skip along the path, further into the gardens.

Mr. Thorne watched after her, a steady look in his eyes.

"It must be terribly difficult for a girl as young as she is to lose her mother," I said.

"It was," Mr. Thorne said. "As I have said, I am not certain that she ever truly recovered. Part of her behavior may be easily traced back to Mrs. Thorne's death."

"How long ago did it happen?" I asked.

"Eight months," Mr. Thorne said. "Though she was sick for much longer than that."

I looked over at him. "What happened?"

He and I began up the path after Miss Elizabeth, away from the beautiful statue of Mrs. Thorne. "She was always a sickly sort of creature. Even when she was young and we were betrothed, it was uncommon for me to see her, as she had to be kept in her room. Her parents knew that our match would be advantageous, especially for her, and the choice had been made before I was even old enough to speak. She was always very kind, and as she grew, she became stronger. Soon, she was able to spend time out of doors, which was unheard of when she was a child. So when we were married and she was with child, all of the doctors were surprised. Some expected her to have difficulty. They were thrilled, and so were we. When she lost two others afterward, though, we began to worry that her health was taking another turn for the worse. Ultimately, that ended up being the truth."

The sun was dipping lower toward the trees in the distance, and as we came around the front of the house, the light danced across the surface of the pond, causing it to shimmer.

"It is rather unfortunate, though, as deaths seems to be following my family these last few years," Mr. Thorne said as we walked.

I felt a small twinge of worry as he said those words. "What do you mean by that?" I asked.

"I lost my brother a few years ago as well," he said. "He was older than I and was to inherit Northington Park himself."

I waited for him to supply more information, and when he didn't, I frowned. "I'm very sorry, Mr. Thorne," I said.

He gave me a tight smile. "You have nothing to apologize for." He took a deep breath, straightening his shoulders. "What's done is done, and there is nothing to be done about it."

I looked away. The whispers of the servants filled my mind, the accusations that Mr. Thorne had been the one to end his own brother's life out of jealousness.

It was hard to believe, hearing the way he so fondly spoke of his late wife, yet was it possible he wished to provide a better life for his sickly wife? It was not that preposterous to imagine, was it?

"Father!" Miss Elizabeth was standing in the drive, pointing excitedly behind her at the carriage that had appeared.

"I wonder who that could be," Mr. Thorne said, taking longer strides toward the house.

We entered the foyer and were greeted by Mr. Gibbs. "Good morning, Mr. Thorne. Your guests are waiting for you in the drawing room."

"Very good," Mr. Thorne said, removing his gloves.

"And they requested the presence of Miss Honeyfield, as well," said Mr. Gibbs.

My heart was once more like a bird trapped in a cage. I looked over at Mr. Thorne.

He smiled at me. "I believe that can be arranged."

9

We climbed the stairs to the first floor, my heart in my throat. Who were these people that had come to call upon Mr. Thorne? And why were they asking me to join them?

I felt a small hand close around my own as we reached the landing. I glanced down to see Miss Elizabeth walking along beside me, her hand in mine.

"Do not be afraid, Miss Honeyfield," she said with a smile. "I shall stay with you so you do not feel alone."

I squeezed her hand. "Thank you, Miss Elizabeth. That makes me feel much better already."

Mr. Thorne was speaking with Mr. Gibbs, too far

ahead for me to hear clearly what they spoke of. Miss Elizabeth seemed all too happy to walk along with me. Perhaps that walk out of doors was all she needed to put her in a brighter mood.

We made it to the drawing room, and Mr. Thorne stepped inside just after Mr. Gibbs. I heard Mr. Gibbs announce Mr. Thorne's arrival.

"And Miss Elizabeth," said Mr. Gibbs as Miss Elizabeth entered the room.

I stepped up to the door, and Mr. Gibbs smiled at me. "And Miss Honeyfield."

I don't believe I was ever formally announced to a room, especially not so soon after the master of the house or his daughter.

I was just about to curtsey when my eyes fell on the couple who were already in the room.

"Lady Hayward," I said, my eyes growing wide.

Aunt Patience smiled up at me from the armchair she sat in, and her husband, my Uncle Charles, nodded at me from behind the chair.

"Oh, there is my dear," Aunt Patience said, holding out her hand to me. "It is so wonderful to see your face again."

I was stunned to silence.

"Miss Honeyfield, you know Lady Hayward?" Miss Elizabeth asked.

"Yes, my dear. She is Miss Honeyfield's aunt," Mr. Thorne said.

Miss Elizabeth's eyes widened. "I had no idea."

"Sir Hayward, I am honored to receive you, especially on such a lovely day," Mr. Thorne said with a bow. "What can a humble man like me do for you?"

"Well, we made a promise to my wife's dear sister's husband that we would go see his eldest daughter and ensure she was well," Sir Hayward said with a smile in my direction. "We have received all of her letters, and it has given Lady Hayward much joy to hear about all that she and Miss Brown have been doing."

"Yes, poor Miss Brown is feeling quite under the weather this morning, or I would introduce you," Mt. Thorne said. "Though I can say with certainty that Miss Honeyfield has been paramount in my daughter's education and happiness."

"Well, isn't that wonderful to hear?" Aunt Patience said with a glint in her eye.

I imagined she was quite pleased to hear that the arrangements she had made for me were working out as well as they were. I could tell from the way she glanced back and forth between Mr. Thorne and me.

"Miss Elizabeth, why don't you tell Lady Hayward how much you are enjoying your music lessons?" Mr. Thorne said, laying a hand on his daughter's shoulder.

Miss Elizabeth smiled and took a step toward my aunt. "Miss Honeyfield is teaching me how to be better player. I have learned so very much from her. She plays wonderfully, and I hope that I can play as well as she can one day." She turned her smiling face toward me, and I recognized the playfulness in her eyes.

I smiled back at her. She meant to tease me, didn't she?

"How wonderful," Sir Hayward said. "I really must thank you again, Mr. Thorne, for taking Miss Honeyfield in. While her father and sisters miss her dearly, his burdens have been lighter, and he knows that she is doing her very best here to take care of her stead and make a difference."

"It was no trouble at all," Mr. Thorne said. "To be quite frank, I am not certain that my house would be the same without her any longer."

Aunt Patience gave a girlish laugh. "Oh, Mr. Thorne, you must be careful, or Miss Honeyfield shall think that you were trying to win her heart."

Mr. Thorne looked over at me, his eyes growing wide.

What a thing for Aunt Patience to say! Of all the forward, impudent, selfish things to say…

I expected to see frustration on his face, or disgrace. I even thought there might be anger toward me, as if he imagined I was the one who orchestrated this whole scenario just for her to say the very thing she just did.

And yet… I saw nothing like that. In fact, I saw a smile. A small smile, yet a smile, nevertheless.

"Mr. Thorne, I hope you do not think that we have come to disrupt your day for nothing more than seeking after the well-being of our niece, though that is of great importance, of course," Sir Hayward said with a smile in my direction.

"Well, Sir, you and Lady Hayward are always welcome in my home, you know that," he said.

"We appreciate it greatly, Mr. Thorne, but we came to discuss the ball that you spoke of earlier this summer," Aunt Patience said.

Miss Elizabeth let out a small gasp. "A ball? Father, you did not tell me you meant to have a ball."

Mr. Thorne nodded. "I do recall saying something about a ball," he said. "Though this summer was so busy that I must admit, I had quite forgotten."

"Oh, Father, we must have a ball before the winter comes," Miss Elizabeth said, grabbing onto her father's arm, gazing up into his eyes. "It will be the cheeriest way to prepare for Christmas, will it not?"

"I daresay it would be," Mr. Thone said.

"And of course, you must invite Miss Honeyfield and her sisters, all of whom are unmarried," Lady Hayward said, lifting her chin into the air ever so slightly. The look she gave Mr. Thorne was somewhat cool look.

I stared at her. How could she ask such a thing of Mr. Thorne? I was nothing more than a tutor. It wasn't as if I was a young woman of a reputable home with any sort of connections to speak of.

"Well, of course," Mr. Thorne said. "I should like to meet Miss Honeyfield's sisters, and her father, as well. I would never deny my Lady the chance to invite her own family." He gave her a bow.

"Wonderful," Aunt Patience said. "When shall we have the ball?"

"I should think a weekend in October would be preferable. What say you, Lady Hayward?" Mr. Thorne asked.

"I believe that will work just splendidly," Sir Hayward said. "What of the first Saturday? We could celebrate the harvest, and I could send some of my chefs along to help prepare the meal. How many guests would you like to invite?"

The conversation carried on for some time, working out various details about the ball. Miss Elizabeth, as well as my aunt, seemed to be the most excited.

"Thank you very much, Mr. Thorne, for your gracious hospitality," Aunt Patience said. "Though I wondered if it might be possible for Sir Hayward and I to speak with our niece about some private matters?"

My face flooded with color. What sort of private matters did she have in mind?

"Certainly, my lady," Mr. Thorne said. "That shall be no trouble at all. Miss Elizabeth, if you would follow me, we can allow Lady Hayward a chance to speak with Miss Honeyfield."

Miss Elizabeth turned and gave me a longing sort of look.

"I won't be long," I said to her, smiling.

She nodded and took her father's hand, who lead her from the room.

Mr. Gibbs also stepped out of the room with a bow, closing the door behind himself.

"Well, now, dear, how are you doing?" Aunt

Patience asked. "Don't be shy. You can come sit over here beside me."

Nervously, I made my way over to the chair next to Aunt Patience's. It was a chair I had never sat in before.

"Come now," she said, patting the arm affectionately.

I sat, though I was careful to keep my back straight as she always taught me and folded my hands in my lap.

"You are doing well, it seems," Uncle Charles said with a smile. "We are very pleased to see this."

"Yes, indeed," Aunt Patience said. "Tell me, my dear, are you happy here? You may speak freely now that Mr. Thorne and Miss Elizabeth are gone."

"I am quite content here, yes," I said. "Mr. Thorne has been very kind to me, and I find teaching Miss Elizabeth invigorating. It has been some time since I was able to enjoy music as much as I have in these last few months."

"That's very good," Uncle Charles said.

"This ball, though…" I said, looking over at Aunt Patience. "Why did you insist on my attendance? That was quite unorthodox, insisting that someone who may as well be a servant be allowed to attend, as well as the rest of her poor family."

"You are still an unmarried young woman, my dear," Aunt Patience said. "Why should you be deprived of the chance to meet single men just because you are working for Mr. Thorne now?"

What could she possibly be thinking now?

"The only reason why you were able to ask such things of him was because he would never dare defy a request of my uncle," I said, my eyes narrowing.

"Well, of course, my dear," Aunt Patience said. "But if we are to ensure that you or any of your sisters are to be married, then we must ensure that you have every possible opportunity to meet these young men. That is the only logical course of action, wouldn't you agree?"

I folded my arms and looked away, my face turning pink.

"How else would you suggest your sister Amelia meet a man?" Aunt Patience asked, her tone becoming rather cool. "Perhaps in passing when she goes into town for your father?"

"No, I realize that these events are important," I said. "Yet I cannot help but feel you manipulated poor Mr. Thorne for your own gains."

"And what of your relationship with Mr. Thorne?" Aunt Patience asked. "He's quite a handsome man, is he not?"

I stared at her, my heart beginning to race. I had never considered Mr. Thorne as handsome, for I had never given myself a chance to truly notice one way or another.

"And quite amiable," Sir Hayward said. "Not to mention he is in need of a wife, as his first wife passed away just last year."

"Yes, I am aware," I said.

"Poor Miss Elizabeth needs a mother," Aunt Patience said, giving me a very pointed look.

My eyes widened. "And you mean for me to fill that role?"

Aunt Patience shrugged. "And whyever not?" she asked. "You are a very amiable young woman, and it is quite clear that his daughter already adores you, yes?"

I could not believe what I was hearing. "Was this your purpose all along?" I asked.

"And if it was part of my motivation?" Aunt Patience said.

"How would a man like Mr. Thorne ever notice me? A woman who was teaching his daughter how to play the piano? I have no value to offer anyone," I said.

"And what if the man has all the value for the both of you?" Aunt Patience asked.

I scoffed, rising from my chair and walking across the room.

"You cannot tell me that you have not considered this already?" Aunt Patience said.

"No, I have not considered it," I said. "I came to teach Miss Elizabeth, not to find a husband."

"Well, you are letting yourself down then, my dear," Aunt Patience said. "Truly, you are missing a wonderful opportunity."

"Your aunt is right," Uncle Charles said. "Mr. Thorne would be a very good match for you."

I looked away. Were they not aware of the rumors that seemed to echo around this home from the lips of the servants?

"We shall not pressure you any further," Aunt Patience said. "Though it seems we have planted the idea in Mr. Thorne's mind. I believe my hint will have been enough."

"That hint may as well have been a discussion of my dowry," I said.

"You worry too much, my dear," Aunt Patience said.

The truth was, I wondered if perhaps I did not worry enough.

10

I woke in the middle of the night after having a rather troubling dream. It was dark, and I heard the voice of my sister Amelia over and over again. She would call to me from a room down the hall at Northington Park. As I attempted to find her, she would suddenly be across the hall. No matter what I did, I could never find her.

I made my way to the door that Mr. Thorne kept private, following my sister's voice on the other side.

When I pushed the door open, I found a shadowed body prostrate on the ground, and before the scream left my mouth, I awoke.

My face was damp with cold sweat, and the air in the room was stale. I threw open the window and drank in mouthfuls of the bitter night air.

Even still, I knew I would be unable to go back to sleep easily. I decided the best way for me to calm down would be to warm myself up with a hot cup of tea.

I lit a candle from my bedside table and made my way out into the hall.

The house itself was extremely quiet. I heard no sounds apart from the window against the windows and the ticking of the clock in the hall.

It was calming to walk through the halls and not hear the voice of my sister. Awake, I realized how strange it would have been to hear her voice in the first place. But the image of the person on the floor of Mr. Thorne's room... It still sent shivers down my back.

As I neared the main stairwell, a draft swept through the landing and snuffed out the light of my candle, submerging me in complete darkness.

I could not see a thing. Every sound made me jump, all the small hairs on my arms standing up straight.

I had two choices. I could continue to the kitchens, where I would easily be able to find a new candle or some spare matches, or I could turn around and make my way back up to my room through the dark. In relation to either room, I was certainly much closer to the kitchens, yet I was not entirely confident about my ability to make it there without error.

I gripped the railing of the stairwell, willing myself to calm down.

I was never afraid of very much as a child, but the darkness almost made me believe that I was alone. When I was tucked away in bed, those thoughts never seemed to trouble me. Yet here I stood in the middle of this great manor, entirely alone, with several hours until sunrise.

What was I to do?

I reprimanded myself, knowing that I was acting like a child. It would do me no good to stand there like I was, so frightened I was unable to move. The only way for me to ensure I would be able to get any more sleep that night would be to finish my journey.

I knew part of my hesitancy was due to those terrible dreams I had. It was not often that I was shaken by such things, but things often seemed more unreal in the middle of the night.

Determined, I took a step forward down the stairs. Perhaps I would find another match in the foyer. Or it was possible that someone else was awake, and I might see light as I moved further into the house.

I carried on down the stairs, which seemed to go on forever... until I tripped over something and fell the rest of the way down.

My legs gave way underneath me, and desperately as I tried, I was unable to catch myself on the railing. Instead, a great pain rose from my foot as I rolled down the last few steps onto the cold marble floor of the landing.

It took me a moment to realize the world around me had stopped spinning. It only took another moment after that to feel the soft, bushy tail of one of the cook's larder cats against my arm, apparently seeking affection.

Or perhaps it was an apology.

"Ow..." I said, attempting to sit up. My arms felt all right, as did my head. But my foot... I knew without even trying that I would not be able to stand on it.

My heart began to race once more. What was I to do? Would someone find me lying here in the morning after a night on the cold, hard floor?

A light at the top of the stairs drew my eye.

"What's happened?" came a familiar voice. "Who is down there?"

"Mr. Thorne," I said. "It's me, Miss Honeyfield."

Frantic footsteps hurried down the stairs, the

warm light of a lit candle coming nearer. "Miss Honeyfield. What happened? Are you all right?"

"I am not sure," I said. "It's my ankle, sir. I cannot stand on it."

His face came swimming into view, heavily shadowed in the light of the candle. "May I?" he asked, setting the candlestick down onto the stair beside me.

I nodded.

He reached out and gently touched my foot, which was bare.

I very nearly kicked out but did my best to control myself. He was doing it to help me, nothing more.

"I see no wound," he said. "Is it your right ankle?"

"Yes, sir," I said.

He had barely touched my skin, yet a great shiver rose up through my spine. "I see. Yes, it is rather swollen. Come, I shall help you stand, and we shall go to the kitchens where I may warm up some water to ease the pain."

In one quick movement, his arm was around my waist, and he lifted me into the air as if I weighed nothing at all.

"Mr. Thorne, I—" I said, throwing my arms around his neck, frightful.

"Did I hurt you?" he asked, a nervous color in his tone.

"No, I am quite all right," I said, breathless. "You simply surprised me."

"My apologies," he said.

And we started toward the kitchens after he picked up his candle and gave it to me to hold.

"What on earth are you doing out of bed so late at night?" he asked.

"You will think me no better than a child," I said. "I had some rather troubling dreams, and when I woke, I thought I might come make myself some tea. My candle blew out from a draft in the room, and as I attempted to continue down the stairs, I tripped over one of Mr. Able's cats, and that was where you chanced upon me."

"I don't believe it to be chance when I heard your frightened cry from down the hall," he said. "I was up myself, unable to sleep. I thought I heard someone in distress, so I came out to see. I am certainly glad I did."

"As am I, sir," I said. "I worried I would not be found until morning."

When we reached the kitchen, he walked inside

and set me gently down on a bench beside the fireplace, which was nothing more than glowing coals.

"Wait right here," he said.

I watched as he walked across the kitchen and found some matches with which to light a few more candles, giving the room a brighter glow. Then, he set down a candle beside me before turning and lifting some logs from the rack beside the door.

"Oh, Mr. Thorne, it's quite all right, you do not need to go to all the trouble," I said.

But he ignored me and tossed the logs inside the hearth.

I soon found I was rather astounded at Mr. Thorne's skills. Fire making was something the cook and the servants did, not the master of the house. Yet here he was, kneeling beside the now glowing flames, a fire poker in his hands to shift the logs around.

"That should do it," he said, getting to his feet and dusting the ash from his knees. "I shall put the kettle on, and you shall have your tea. How is your ankle?"

"It's quite all right, sir," I said.

He turned and raised an eyebrow at me, his hands on his hips. "Can you stand on it?" he asked.

I looked away. "Of that I am not certain."

He nodded and turned around, locating some cups and some clean linens.

I watched him work for a moment, my mind moving very quickly. Where was this monster the servants seemed to see? How was it possible that someone capable of murder would also be so kind and so gentle?

Not for the first time, I doubted those rumors, and found great peace in doing so.

Setting the kettle on its hook over the fire, he came to sit beside me on the bench. "So, dear Miss Honeyfield. I am curious as to what sort of dreams could frighten you."

My eyes widened and I looked quickly away. "Oh, it was nothing, Mr. Thorne. I can hardly remember it."

"You most certainly can," he said. "I can see by your frightened expression."

I swallowed rather hard, my hands grasping the folds of my dressing gown. "It was... my sister, sir. She was lost, and I was trying to find her, and..." I did not have the heart to finish the thought.

"I see," he said. "I imagine you must miss your family greatly."

"I do, on occasion," I said. "However, I know they go on well without me."

"Yet that tells me nothing of how you feel," he said.

"What I feel matters little," I said rather plainly. "I did what I must, and I do not regret it."

He gave me a searching look, and for a moment, I found myself deeply curious as to what he saw. "I must admit, Miss Honeyfield. I am rather curious as to why you chose to come and live here to work with my daughter instead of perhaps getting married yourself?"

The question was rather poignant, yet it certainly was not the first time hearing it.

"Forgive me if I overstep my bounds, but I am well aware how difficult it can be for a governess, or a tutor much like a governess, to find a match," he said.

"The answer is quite simple, really," I said, my eyes downcast into the fire. "I never expected to receive an offer of marriage. That's all."

He seemed taken aback by that statement; his silence spoke volumes.

I looked around at him. "And if I was not to be suited for marriage, then at least I could be doing something worthwhile with my time."

"I understand your family may not have had as many opportunities as most, yet I cannot understand why someone would be blind to how kind and sensible you are," he said. "Why, the kindness you have shown dear Elizabeth alone has convinced me of this."

"To be quite honest, Mr. Thorne, I am unperturbed by my lack of offers," I said. "Perhaps I was when I was younger, before I realized that being the daughter of a very poor clergyman would not allow for proper interactions in society. Now, do not get me wrong, Mr. Thorne. I love my family dearly and would not trade anything for it, but the truth of the matter is that my sisters and I would have had difficulties finding husbands regardless of how lovely any of us were, or how well accomplished. Our aunt had seen to that when we were younger, even going so far as to holding a ball for each of us so that we may properly come out into society."

I brushed some ash from my own skirt, forcing a smile.

"I am not troubled, though, sir. I am quite pleased with the way my life has turned out in the end. Miss Elizabeth is a wonderful charge, and I feel very honored to be the one helping her to learn more of what she already loves so dearly," I said.

"I understand your reasoning, Miss Honeyfield, but your words feel practiced, as if you have told them to yourself so many times that you have finally come to believe them yourself," he said, rising to his feet and crossing to the now roiling kettle.

I stared at his back, my face draining of color.

"Sir?" I asked. "I fear you are mistaken."

"I know I most certainly am not," he said. "A woman's worth is not in her father's position alone. Any good man with any sense would understand that. Love is a far more common reason for marriage these days, especially when a fortunate young man finds a woman to whom he wishes to pledge his life. That is the sort of woman worth marrying, whether she be the daughter of a dame or a dairy maid." He looked at me pointedly. "And I believe you know this to be true, yet you have allowed yourself to hold steadfast to the contrary."

"Sir, it was not as if I had made acquaintance with a great number of men," I said. "How was I to meet these suitors when they were all attending fine balls and dinner parties, of which I had no part?"

"You think too poorly of yourself, Miss Honeyfield," Mr. Thorne said. "I should like you to see yourself as you truly are."

He poured me some tea and dampened a cloth with the hot liquid, giving it a moment or two to cool before draping it around my ankle.

"There now," he said. "I shall call the doctor in the morning, and he shall look at it properly."

"I think I am quite all right," I said. "You have taken great care of me. I do not deserve it."

"You deserve it," he said. "And a great deal more, for that matter."

Finding I was indeed able to stand, he walked with me back to up to my room where he bade me good night. I found myself unable to wrap my mind around Mr. Thorne and his kindness, and yet I knew there was still a secret that he was hiding. And that secret was enough to put some distance between us in my mind, even when new thoughts of husbands and marriage had unwillingly begun to arise in my thoughts once again, after long since being dormant.

11

The next morning as I was having breakfast with Miss Brown, who was feeling a great deal better finally, Mr. Gibbs entered the room to announce the post had arrived.

"And a letter has come for you, Miss Honeyfield," he said, handing the folded parchment to me.

"Thank you, Mr. Gibbs," I said, smiling up at him.

"Oh, how wonderful, a letter from my cousin Edmund down at the seaside," Miss Brown said, unfolding a letter she held in her hand. "He's quite the amusing fellow. His poor children seem to be taking after him. Ah, yes, it is good to hear that his wife, dear Mrs. Randall, is doing quite all right. She was under a great deal of distress with her most recent pregnancy, but it seems the baby was delivered without difficulty."

"That is wonderful news," I said as I peeled off the wax seal from the back of my letter.

"Who writes to you?" Miss Brown asked, lifting her tea to her lips.

"It seems to be my eldest sister's handwriting," I said. "I suppose she means to tell me about…"

As my eyes skimmed the page, the words faded on my lips.

"Is everything all right, dear?" Miss Brown asked. "You have suddenly gone quite pale."

Dear Sister,

I should very much like to send good news to you, but unfortunately, I am unable to at this time. I hope this letter arrives swiftly, for our youngest sister has taken ill with a rather troubling fever. Father is doing his best not to worry, but Isabella and I worry that it seems all too similar to the same illness that drove our poor mother to her death.

"Miss Honeyfield? Whatever is the matter?" Miss Brown asked.

I looked up at her, my hands beginning to tremble. "My… sister, it seems, has taken ill," I said.

Miss Brown eyes widened. "Taken ill?" she asked.

"From the look on your face, I would assume it is not good news."

I dipped my head once more and continued reading.

Father will not be happy I sent this news to you; he would rather you not have anything to worry about. But I am worried, Juliana. She has not risen out of bed in days, and you know as well as I that Father has not the means to pay for a proper physician. We are doing our best to keep her comfortable, but I shall worry if this continues.

I shall send news as soon as anything changes, for the better... or worse, as much as I hate writing it. Isabella is calling me now. I must fetch some cool towels for Susannah. Oh, Juliana, I had so dearly hoped to never have to do this again...

At the very bottom, she hastily had signed her name, and from a short glance at the wax seal, she had been hurried in that matter, as well.

"I do not know," I said, turning the letter over. "It is dated three days ago. What if she is worse by now? What if she dies, and I will not know until the letter arrives too late?"

Miss Brown was up from her chair in an instant, around the table, and pulling me into her arms like a mother embracing her child. "There, now, it does no good to allow fear to consume one's mind," she said, stroking my hair.

"My father cannot pay a physician," I said. "It will be just the same as what happened with my poor mother."

Miss Brown pulled away from me, staring at me intently. "Miss Honeyfield, you must take this news to Mr. Thorne. Perhaps he can arrange for you to get back to your family before she becomes any worse."

A new fear appeared to cover the others I was already feeling. "Oh, I cannot bother him with such trifles. I… I shall have to ask his permission to leave, of course. But I could walk the ten miles in one day, especially if I were to leave soon."

"Come with me," Miss Brown said, latching her hand around my wrist and dragging me from the room.

We wandered down the hall for a moment like a mother pulling her child, when a stern-looking woman stepped through the door of the parlor.

"Mrs. Frampton, have you seen Mr. Thorne this morning?" Miss Brown asked.

Mrs. Frampton's sour expression deepened. "I most certainly have. What might you need with him?"

"Miss Honeyfield must speak with him," Miss

Brown said. "It is a matter of emergency."

Mrs. Frampton's eyes narrowed to slits. "Upon my word, I have never heard of such impertinence."

"Mrs. Frampton, please," I said. "I just received news that my youngest sister is very ill. I need to get back to see her."

I kept eye contact with her for a long moment, determined not to look away.

It seemed to work, for she sighed and looked away. "He is taking breakfast," she said, and with her nose in the air, she made her way down the hall.

Miss Brown and I hurried down the stairs to the breakfast room. We hurried inside, both bowing as we did so.

"Well, what a pleasant surprise," Mr. Thorne said, lowering his newspaper. "Look, dear Elizabeth. Your instructors have come to see us. But look here, why are your faces so long, dear ladies?"

Miss Brown gave me a sidelong look out of her eye.

I took a deep breath and stepped forward. "Sir, I have just received news that my youngest sister has taken ill."

"Good heavens," he said, his tone gentler and more reserved. "This is serious, then, is it?"

I nodded, willing the tears that threatened to

come to not do so, but my vision blurred, and I found it difficult to look at him. "Yes, sir. She is just turned nineteen, and my sister believes it could be the very same illness that took my mother from us."

Mr. Thorne stood at once, his paper abandoned. "Then there is no time to lose," he said. "I shall call for the carriage, and we shall be on our way at once."

All thoughts of tears disappeared as I gaped up at him. "Mr. Thorne?"

"I'm sorry, dear Elizabeth, but I shall be leaving you in the care of your dear Miss Brown for a few days, if that is all right."

Miss Elizabeth appeared as shocked as I was, her blue-green eyes wide as she stared at him. "But how long will you be gone for?"

"Hopefully, no more than a day or two," he said. "I shall write as soon as we arrive. Remember, Miss Honeyfield's home is only a short ten miles from here. If anything was to happen, I could be back in just a few hours."

Miss Elizabeth turned her round eyes on me. "She is your sister?" she asked.

Moved by her fear, as well as my own, I walked around the side of the table and knelt down beside her, taking her hand in my own. "Dear, sweet, Elizabeth… yes. She is my sister. And she is much too young to be ill. I must go and help her get well again." I hoped with every ounce of faith within me that she would, indeed, become well once more.

Miss Elizabeth searched my face for a long, hard moment. "And I shan't come with you?" she asked.

I shook my head. "No, my dear. I fear that this trip will be more for work than for play. I promise you, the next time I am to return home for a visit, you shall come with me."

A smile grew across her innocent face. "And you shall show me the flower fields where you played as a girl?"

"Indeed," I said. "If there are any in bloom, I shall bring them home for you."

Miss Elizabeth nodded. "And... you shall come back to Northington Park, yes? I should miss you if you were to go away forever."

I leaned forward and kissed her on the forehead. "I shall return," I said. "You have my word, dear one."

Miss Elizabeth smiled at me and then turned to her father. "Please do not be gone long, Father. I shall miss you both when you are away."

"And my heart shall pine for you, my dear," he said. "I will come and say goodbye before we depart."

It was a whirlwind after leaving the breakfast room. Mr. Thorne instructed me to get packed as quickly as I could. Miss Brown entreated me to help, and we gathered some clothes and other necessities into my small suitcase to take with me.

"Take these," Miss Brown said, hurrying back into my room, her arm laden with various articles. "New dresses, some healing herbs, some books on prayer, though I am certain your father must have every one of these," she said, tucking them all inside. "And please, Miss Honeyfield, do not despair. You will see your sister, and your presence alone will likely cause her to perk up with joy."

"I hope you are right," I said. "I fear we may be too late."

"Do not give the devil so much room," Miss Brown said. "Remain at peace. You shall save your strength that way."

Mr. Gibbs carried my suitcase down to the foyer for me, where Mr. Thorne was instructing Mrs. Frampton on things before leaving.

"Ah, there you are, Miss Honeyfield," Mr. Thorne said. "Thank you, Mrs. Frampton," he said as an aside to the stoic woman. He turned back to me. "Are we ready?"

"Yes, indeed, sir," I said.

"Very good," he said, offering his arm to me, and we strode out the door together.

The footman helped me into the carriage, and I didn't even have a chance to look before Mr. Thorne had climbed up beside me, pulling the door closed behind him.

He pulled his hat from his head, turning to look at me. "How are you feeling?"

"A bit nervous," I said. "How long before we arrive?"

"I imagine just before dinner," he said, gazing out the window. "As long as the rain holds out on us."

I suppressed a shiver. I hoped the weather would not delay us.

The carriage began to move, and its jostling was soothing to me, reminding me that we were on our way much faster than I would be if I had chosen to walk instead.

"I cannot thank you enough, Mr. Thorne, for allowing me to ride in your carriage back to my home," I said.

"You are quite welcome," he said. "I don't believe there is anyone more deserving than you, if I'm honest."

My face turned scarlet. I was glad for the bonnet

I wore to cover my face.

"I should have you know that I have also written to my friend, Dr. Williams, and asked him to meet us at your home. I informed him of the situation and have already sent one of my errand boys to town with it. He should be there shortly after we arrive."

"Oh, Mr. Thorne, you are doing far too much for my family," I said. "You really shouldn't have done such a thing. For there is no earthly way for my father to pay you apart from his deepest gratitude."

"And that shall be quite enough," Mr. Thorne said. "I trust Dr. Williams greatly. He is Miss Elizabeth's physician, after all."

That thought was deeply comforting as we rode through the countryside.

"I am pleased Miss Elizabeth agreed to let us go," I said.

"I am as well," he said. "I feared she might have one of her great tantrums. You know how little she likes her routine disrupted." He nodded his head. "It seems there is some maturing happening in the heart of my daughter. This is an unexpected development, yet I must admit that I am rather pleased to recognize it." He looked over at me. "And I imagine that your pleading with her helped her to feel as if she had part in the decision. You were very kind to her, and I was pleased to hear that she seemed more concerned with your return than my leaving in the first place."

"That surprised me as well," I said. "Almost as much as your insistence to accompany me in the first place."

"I could not very well allow you to travel this far alone," he said. "And like you, we have both lost loved ones to sickness like this. You should not have to endure this alone."

The paramount reality was not on me in those moments. The master of the house had agreed to travel with me, a lowly tutor to his daughter, to ensure that my sister was well taken care of. It did not seem possible, or even likely, that something like this would happen. Yet here we were, well on our way to my father's parsonage.

I did my best not to dwell on it, though, instead choosing to keep my thoughts on my sister and instead be grateful to Mr. Thorne for his graciousness in the first place.

And though it was harder to do, I did my best to subdue the hope rising in my heart that there was something indeed very different about Mr. Thorne... and that I should like to become more familiar with him.

12

I began to recognize the countryside as the sun began to dip toward the horizon. Farms belonging to family friends appeared on the horizon, as well as the small town where my father gave his sermons every Sunday morning.

The carriage pulled into the narrow drive of the small cottage that my family owned just as the sunbeams were obscured behind the trees.

My heart clenched in my chest. The house was far smaller than even I remembered it. How could I have forgotten? A window in one of the bedrooms was cracked, and the hinge along the door was coming loose. The flagstone path leading to the front door was uneven, and the ivy growing along the eastern side had completely obscured the window into the sitting room.

Embarrassment caused my cheeks to flush, yet I held my chin high.

"Come along, Miss Honeyfield. There is no time to waste," Mr. Thorne said as the carriage came to a stop.

I allowed him to help me out, and I swept toward the front door, my thoughts entirely focused on my poor sister who I hoped was still doing all right.

I knocked on the door and heard commotion on the other side. It wasn't a moment later before it swung inward and I saw the face of my sister, Isabella, staring out at me.

Her eyes grew wide, her mouth falling open. "Juliana...?" she asked, clutching her hand over her heart. "Oh, my heavens!" she said, her face splitting into a smile. She threw herself across the threshold into my arms, laughing.

I staggered a little under her embrace, returning her affection for but a moment before peeling her off of me. "Isabella, where is Susannah?"

"She's in bed, of course," Isabella said, a more serious expression passing over her face. "Is that why you're here? Did Amelia write to you?"

"Yes, she did," I said. "And I came as soon as I received the letter."

Isabella's eyes fell upon Mr. Thorne, who stood behind me, and she gave me a questioning look.

"This is Mr. Thorne," I said, gesturing to him. "Mr. Thorne, this is my middle sister, Miss Isabella Honeyfield."

Her eyes widened until I feared they might fall directly out of her head. "Mr. Thorne, what a pleasure it is to meet you," she said, lowering herself into a curtsy, and hiding her face.

"The pleasure is mine, I assure you," he said. "Is your father home?"

"Why, yes, sir, he is," Isabella said. "Please, come inside."

The subtle scent of freshly baked bread and my mother's favorite, lavender, hung in the air as I stepped inside. A wave of emotion washed over me, and I had not been prepared for it. I tried to hide my sudden influx of sorrow mingled with longing as we made our way toward the sitting room.

"Father, you will not believe who has come to visit," said Isabella as she stepped into the room. "My dear sister, and her employer, Mr. Thorne."

I crossed the threshold after her, my eyes searching for my father's face at once. I located it in his chair beside the fire. It was clear they had just finished dinner; a half-played game of cards was out on the table, and a tea kettle was sitting beside three partially finished cups.

"My heavens…" Father said, rising to his feet, his eyes as wide as Isabella's had been. "What on earth are you doing back here?"

"I came as soon as I received Amelia's letter," I said. "Where is Susannah?"

"In her room, of course," Father said. "Amelia is tending to her now." He turned his gaze onto Mr. Thorne, who smiled down at him. "And you, sir. I am humbled by your appearance. It is an honor and a great pleasure to meet you." He bowed deeply.

"You, sir, have my deepest respect," Mr. Thorne said. "Being a clergyman is a thankless task, and I am well acquainted with it."

"Are you?" Father asked. "Perhaps a relative of yours?"

"My uncle," he said. "The kindest man I know. As you must be, for there is no one quite as kind, or as sensible, as your eldest daughter."

"I am indebted to you for what you have done for my daughter," Father said, stooping into a bow once again. "Please, can I get you anything? Perhaps some tea?"

"No, that is quite all right, sir," Mr. Thorne said.

"Father, may we see her?" I asked him, impatient to wait any longer.

"Of course," Father said, motioning toward the staircase through the narrow doorway.

"I do hope you do not think me too forward, sir, but I have asked a dear friend of mine, a Dr. Williams, to come by here and check on your daughter," Mr. Thorne said.

I heard the nervousness in Father's voice at once. "Oh, sir, I beg you. You are far too generous. I could not possibly accept such an offer, it is far too kind."

"Call it the personal favor of a friend," Mr. Thorne said. He laid a hand on my father's shoulder. "I lost my wife to sickness as well, Mr. Honeyfield. I daresay it would do my heart good to know that you shall not lose anyone else in the same fashion."

I hurried into Susannah's room, the room she shared with Isabella, and found her sprawled out on her bed, the blankets pulled up to her chin.

"Oh, dear sister," I said, my heart caught in my throat.

Amelia, who was sitting in the chair beside the bed with her needle and thread, gazed up at me as if she could not believe her eyes. "Juliana!" she exclaimed, jumping to her feet. "What are you doing

—" Her words faded as Mr. Thorne and Father stepped into the room behind me.

"Dear sister," Susannah said from the bed. She lifted her head and made to sit up.

"No, do not move on my account," I said, hurrying over to her to ease her gently back down onto the bed. "It's all right. Amelia sent me a letter and said that you were ill, so I came as soon as I could."

Susannah gave Amelia a rather incredulous look. "What did you say to her that caused her to run over here as quickly as she possibly could?"

Amelia's cheeks flushed pink. "I simply told her that you had fallen ill quite suddenly, and that it reminded me of when Mother became so sick, and—"

Susannah collapsed against her pillows with a groan. "Amelia, you frightened her half to death!"

"I am sorry!" Amelia said. "But at the time, you were so unwell, and it frightened me because Mother became ill so quickly, too."

Susannah shook her head. "Juliana, there was no need for you to come. It is nothing more than a cold. My fever has all but passed, and I am mending. Amelia seems to have allowed her fear to get the better of her and not her good sense to govern her actions," she said, glaring at Amelia. She then glanced up at me. "I am sorry to trouble you so, sister. Though I am quite flattered to see the depth of your affection for me."

I squeezed her hand affectionately.

"Well, it isn't as if you are up and dancing, though, is it?" Mr. Thorne said. "These sorts of illnesses still must be taken very seriously. When Dr. Williams arrives, he shall give you a thorough examination to ensure that you are healing well enough."

Susannah's eyes snapped to Amelia once more. "Did you hear that, sister? A doctor is coming to call on me. All because of you. Juliana, do you see what has happened to us in your absence?"

"Do not get so overworked, sister," I said, patting Susannah's hand affectionately. "Otherwise you surely will aggravate that fever."

"Father, someone is at the door," came Isabella's voice from downstairs.

"I imagine that would be the good doctor," Mr. Thorne said with a smile.

I followed him from the room, my heart beating rather erratically. "Mr. Thorne, I feel I must apologize for my sister's negligence," I said. "If I had known that the situation was not nearly as dire as she had made me to believe, then—"

"It's quite all right, Miss Honeyfield," he said. "It is always better to err on the side of caution, is it not? I, for one, am quite relieved to find her on the mend, for it could have quite easily been the opposite."

"Indeed," I said. "I am simply ashamed that you have come all this way for such an insignificant thing."

He stopped suddenly in the narrow hall to look down at me.

I nearly bumped into him.

"Things that are important are never insignificant," he said in a low voice. "Least of all those we love."

I was shortly thereafter introduced to Dr. Williams, who was a very amiable gentleman with great knowledge and experience. His thinning white hair gave him a gentle expression, and he seemed all too happy to attend to Susannah.

I waited outside her door while the doctor gave her diagnosis. He also deemed it nothing more than a cold that should pass with plenty of rest and some hearty meals to strengthen her when she felt up to it. He also gave her some herbs to add to her tea to soothe her aches and settle her stomach and promised to be back within the week to check in on her once again.

I breathed a great sigh of relief and made my way back downstairs where Father and Mr. Thorne were waiting.

"...so late after all, I cannot imagine you would wish to travel at this hour," Father was saying. "You would, of course, be welcome to stay here for the night."

I felt my breath catch, and I hesitated just outside the room, awaiting Mr. Thorne's answer. Now that the danger had passed, the truth was, we had nowhere to go that evening.

"That is a very generous offer, Mr. Honeyfield, one that I shall gladly accept," he said. "We shall join you for breakfast tomorrow, and then Miss Honeyfield and I shall be on our way back to Northington Park. My daughter will be quite relieved to have us back so soon, especially Miss Honeyfield. Oh, how she does dote on her."

"Wonderful," Father said. "Shall I fetch you something to eat? I imagine you must be hungry after such a long carriage ride over here."

"Perhaps something small would suffice," Mr. Thorne said kindly. "I should not wish to burden you."

"You do no such thing, good sir," Father said. "It is a pleasure having your company."

Father left the room for the kitchen, and I stepped out into the sitting room.

Mr. Thorne turned his eyes toward me, his face set in deep contrast in the dim candlelight.

"Dr. Williams says that Susannah will be fine," I said, taking a seat in a chair at the small, round table. "She needs rest, though, and he said he would return to see her progress in a few days."

"Splendid," Mr. Thorne said. "I am pleased to hear it."

"As am I," I said, smoothing out the wrinkles in the tablecloth. It was one Mother and I had stitched together when I was young; the lilies along the hem had held up nicely over the years, their color only fading slightly.

"Your father has kept a fine home for your sisters," Mr. Thorne said.

"Do not mock me, Mr. Thorne," I said. "You may be my superior, but I shall not have you speak ill of my family."

His eyebrows arched toward his hairline. "My heavens, it seems I have found some passion buried beneath all that sensibility." A smile crept onto his face. "I hope you know I meant no harm in my words. I meant them. Money does not always end in happiness, and just from looking around this quaint cottage, I can see that it was filled with nothing but love. You were quite blessed to have grown up in such a place."

I gave him a steady look, trying to discern the seed of truth hidden amongst his words. "Were you not so fortunate as a child?"

He gave a harsh laugh. "Hardly. My father was not the sentimental type, and my mother seemed more interested in the gossip at her parties. My brother and I were often left to our own devices while they doted on my sisters, all of whom were married off to men of great fortune. In my father's opinion, our fate had been sealed as soon as we were born, and we would never struggle finding a suitable wife. We were raised by our governess, which is why I took such care in finding a good one for Elizabeth." He smiled. "I bore you now, surely."

"Not at all," I said. "I had no idea you thought so little about your upbringing."

"I don't think little of it," he said. "I am simply aware that there are those who were given a great deal more affection than I was, and that I want that for my own family."

"I think that is admirable," I said.

"Thank you," he said. "And I hope your father knows how grateful I am to him for offering us a place to stay for the night. You are all right with this, I assume?"

"Oh, of course," I said. "We shall find room. It will be no trouble at all."

After Dr. Williams left, we spent the next hour or so enjoying a meal with my father, Amelia, and Isabella. Both of my sisters could not seem to keep their eyes off Mr. Thorne, and when the meal had been cleared and Father took Mr. Thorne to the study to show off his book collection, they both turned on me with blaring gazes and pointed stares.

"Sister, you *must* tell us the meaning of this," Isabella said, folding her arms.

"The meaning of what?" I asked as I carried more plates toward the kitchen.

"These long, lingering glances between you and Mr. Thorne, of course," Isabella said, coming quickly behind me.

"There are no such expressions," I said, almost laughing.

"I daresay Isabella is onto something," Amelia said. "He is quite handsome. No one would fault you if you did find him attractive."

"Though I hear him speak of a daughter," Isabella said. "Is he widowed?"

"Yes," I said.

Both Isabella and Amelia gasped.

"You are being ridiculous," I said, turning to them with my hands on my hips.

"Are we, though?" Amelia asked.

"Yes, are we?" Isabella said. "What sort of man would travel all this way with his daughter's tutor just to ensure her sister is well if it was nothing as she believes it to be?"

I stared between them. "I…"

"She hadn't thought of that," Amelia said, her eyes widening.

"There must be something there," Isabella said. "You must admit that you have considered the possibility."

"I am nothing more than a tutor," I said. "And a much older woman than he would surely want in a wife now."

"Yet to hear the way he speaks to you, it isn't as if you are on unequal footing at all," Isabella said. "It is as if he sees you are someone worth knowing."

My face turned scarlet as I did my best to push those thoughts aside.

"What's the matter?" Amelia asked. "You look cross about something."

I glanced over their shoulders out into the sitting room. It seemed Father and Mr. Thorne had not yet returned from the study. I dropped my voice and leaned in toward them. "There are... rumors circulating Northington Park, and I have my fears about them."

I told them quickly what the servants had told me and about how I had seen this room that he was determined to hide.

"I have never seen him look so hardened," I said. "He was certainly being secretive about something."

"If you have questions, then perhaps you should confront him," Isabella said.

"Are you out of your mind?" I asked. "Ask the master of Northington Park if he really did kill his own brother?"

"She's right, you know," Amelia said. "And it isn't as if he would ever admit to it in the first place."

"Precisely," I said.

"Don't you want to know the truth?' Isabella asked.

"Of course I do," I said sharply, my brow furrowed.

"And what do you really think?" Isabella asked. "Do you think a man like Mr. Thorne, who has gone so far out of his way for you, would be capable of something so cruel?"

"You do have a great sense about people, sister," Amelia said. "What say you?"

I only hesitated but a moment. "I don't think he did it," I said.

"Well, then believe it," Isabella said. "And continue to search for the truth if you are so determined."

13

We stayed for breakfast the next morning with my father and sisters. It was a much more lighthearted affair, and I felt confident, yet also somewhat sad, as I waved to them from the carriage window.

"I have great comfort in knowing your sister is doing better," Mr. Thorne said. "As I am certain you are as well."

"Indeed, sir," I said, turning to him. "You have shown such kindness to me. How can I ever thank you for allowing me this great blessing?"

"You owe me nothing," he said. "I feel as if I still owe you a great deal for all the time and effort you have put into the lessons with Elizabeth."

He smiled, yet I saw that it did not quite brighten his face.

"You miss her," I said.

"I do, in fact," he said. "I have been gone from her longer than this before, yet this time feels different for some reason."

"I have missed her, too," I said. "I shall be glad to return to normalcy once again."

We made it back to Northington Park just before dinner, and Miss Elizabeth greeted us at the door with loud shouts of excitement and welcome.

"Father! Miss Honeyfield! You have returned!"

Ignoring a scolding Mrs. Frampton, Miss Elizabeth dashed out of the house toward her father, throwing herself into his arms.

He laughed heartily, picking her up easily and spinning her in the air so her curls swung. "My dear, there you are. My, have you grown in the last few hours?"

She giggled. "Father, you were only gone for one night."

"And that was one night too long," he said, placing her back on her feet on the ground.

Miss Elizabeth then turned her attention to me, her eyes so similar to her father's looking up at me. "Miss Honeyfield," she said, curtsying.

I curtsied in return, trying my best to hide my amusement at her very ladylike behavior.

"How is your sister feeling?" she asked as I knelt down in front of her.

"She is feeling much better now," I said. "Dr. Williams came to see her and promised us all that she needed only rest and some love to get well once again."

Miss Elizabeth nodded. "Dr. Williams is very kind. I like him very much."

"As do I," I said.

"Father, you are just in time for dinner," Miss Elizabeth said, taking his hand in her own.

"Wonderful, for I am famished," he said.

"Thank you again, Mr. Thorne," I said. "I cannot thank you enough."

"You have already," he said with a low laugh.

I curtsied to him as well and started for the stairwell.

"Where are you going, Miss Honeyfield?" he asked.

"Oh, to my room, sir," I said. "I shall return to the kitchens for a meal once I am finished unpacking."

"Why don't you join Miss Elizabeth and me for dinner this evening?" he asked.

I could feel the stares of Mrs. Frampton on the

back of my head, as if I had been the one to ask to dine with them instead of the other way around.

"I... would be honored to," I said.

Mr. Gibbs stared at me as I passed, too. Everyone was just as aware as I was that this was very unconventional, treating me as if I were a guest as opposed to a member of his employed staff.

Mr. Thorne arranged for another seat at the table to be brought up, which the servants obeyed readily. I did my best not to look them in the eye, for I knew they must be wondering the same thing that I was; why was I receiving such special treatment?

"Miss Honeyfield, you need not look so downcast," Mr. Thorne said. "You are my guest this evening, and I do hope that you will enjoy your meal with us."

"Oh, yes, of course," I said. "I shall be glad to."

Miss Elizabeth sat in her seat as patiently as she could, her legs swinging as she looked back and forth between us. "Miss Brown was telling me of the ball," Miss Elizabeth said. "She told me stories last night to help me fall asleep about how wonderful it will all be."

"Ah, yes. I had almost forgotten about this ball of yours," Mr. Thorne said. He turned and looked over at me. "I feel rather foolish now. We were just with your sisters. We certainly missed our opportunity to tell them about the ball, didn't we?"

"We certainly did," I said.

"Will your sisters like to come to the ball?" Miss Elizabeth asked. "Will your sister be well enough?"

"I believe so," I said. "And trust me, my sister Susannah will not miss a ball, even if she would have to dance with a fever."

Miss Elizabeth giggled. "I look forward to meeting your sisters. If they are like you, I am certain I will like them."

"Oh, you certainly will, Elizabeth," Mr. Thorne said. "Her sisters are very amiable young ladies. And Miss Honeyfield could not stop telling them all about you when we were with them, telling them how lovely you were."

Miss Elizabeth turned her large eyes on me. "Did you really, Miss Honeyfield?"

"I certainly did," I said.

"What did you tell them of me?" she asked.

"Well, I told them how wonderfully you played the pianoforte," she said. "I also told them how you were considering taking up the harp, as well. You see, my sister Amelia is rather good at playing the harp, though she does not take great pleasure in it."

Miss Elizabeth's eyes widened. "Whyever not? The harp is such a lovely instrument."

"Indeed it is," I said.

Miss Elizabeth suddenly turned to her father, clutching the table. She gasped. "Father! Will you allow Miss Honeyfield to play at the ball?"

Mr. Thorne turned his attention to me just as the doors to the kitchen opened, and the servants came in with our food. "Well, I certainly think it's a wonderful idea. Miss Honeyfield, what say you?"

"Oh, Mr. Thorne, I am certain you could find a more competent player than I," I said. "I have no experience playing for large crowds, and I am certain I would disappoint you."

"And I am quite certain there is nothing you could do that would disappoint me," Mr. Thorne said. "In any regard."

I met his gaze as one of the servants laid a plate of food in front of me, the aroma tantalizing, reminding me how very little I had eaten that day. But it was not enough to pull me away from his eyes.

He meant something more with his words. I couldn't quite put my finger on what it might be, but he did not simply mean my ability to play music.

"Oh, please, Miss Honeyfield, you must play at the ball," Miss Elizabeth said. "You play better than anyone else I have ever heard. And it would be such a pleasure for everyone else to hear you play, as well."

"She is right, you know," Mr. Thorne said.

I smiled. "Well… All right," I said. "I suppose I will do my very best to live up to your expectations."

"Father, you must ensure that Miss Honeyfield has a new dress, as well," Miss Elizabeth said.

My eyes widened as I stared across the table at her. It was one thing to ask me to play for the ball, but it was entirely different to ask her father to pay for a dress for me. That was out of line, and I could not imagine her father would tolerate her asking something so flippantly as well.

"A new dress, you say?" her father asked, a smile tugging at the corner of his mouth. "Well, if she is to provide us all with some entertainment at the ball, then I suppose the very least I could do is ensure that she has a lovely dress to wear for it."

"But, sir, you are already doing a great deal for me by allowing me to come to the ball in the first place," I said. "A dress would be far too much."

"I appreciate your opinion, Miss Honeyfield, but I believe a dress is a small thing to be concerned about. I shall send for the seamstress in the morning, and we shall have one made especially for you," he said.

I opened my mouth to argue, but he gave me a leveling look.

"I meant what I said," he said. "And I have made up my mind."

I was not entirely sure I believed him until Mr. Gibbs appeared in the school room the next morning just as Miss Elizabeth was beginning her lessons with Miss Brown, alerting me to the fact that the seamstress was there to see me.

With a wide-eyed look at Miss Brown, who simply smiled at me, I was ushered from the room to my Elizabeth's quarters, where I was measured for my dress, as well as asked a few questions about my preference of style. I was in shock that it was happening in the first place, but I did my best to maintain my composure.

It was only a few days later when the seamstress returned with my dress, all finished and ready for me to wear.

With trembling hands, I touched the incredibly beautiful ivory fabric. It was lined with lace around the bodice, and silk ribbons adorned the back. Some shimmering satin had been sewn into the sleeves, and it was so soft and soothing beneath my fingers.

"I have never seen its equal," I said breathlessly to the seamstress.

"I'm glad to hear it, my dear," she said. "Let us see how it fits."

I had always sewn my own clothing, ever since I was a girl. Mother had always ensured that our clothes fit, but never in my life had I worn a dress that fit me as well as this new dress Mr. Thorne had purchased for me did.

I stepped out from behind the dressing screen, unable to take my hands from the skirts, afraid that if I were to blink, I might wake from a wonderful dream I was having.

"Come here, dear, let us see you in front of the mirror," the seamstress said.

My heart was pounding as I stepped in front of the mirror, and the seamstress let out a small laugh.

"My heavens, my dear. It was as if you were made to wear this dress. Don't you think?" she asked.

I couldn't take my eyes from it. From myself. I could not believe that the woman standing in front of the mirror was me.

"I have never felt so beautiful," I said, my eyes stinging with tears.

"Oh, my dear, you should not be so hard on yourself," she said. "You are a lovely woman. I believe you will enjoy your time at the ball. There shall not be a man in the room who can keep his eyes off you."

And with that, I realized there really was only one man that I hoped would find me as lovely as I felt.

14

"Oh, dear sister, I never would have believed it. A ball! And we are in attendance!"

It was a beautiful night. The stars outside were bright and many in number. The sky itself was velvety black without a cloud to be seen. For late October, the air was mild, as well, and there had been no sign of rain for days, leaving everyone in a much more pleasant mood.

"I am very pleased you are so happy, Amelia," I said, smiling at her.

Isabella was staring around the ballroom, her hands tightly wrapped around Amelia's arm. "If I had not seen it with my own eyes, I would never have imagined it could be so beautiful."

"And your dress, sister," Susannah said, giving me a very pointed look. "I have never seen you in anything so fine."

"To be honest, I do not see another woman with a dress as fine as that one," Amelia said with a grin.

"And to think, your Mr. Thorne was the one to purchase it for you," said Isabella with a twirl of her curled hair.

"As I have said, he said it was necessary since I was to play this evening," I said. "He could not very well have a woman play with anything less than the very best to wear."

Isabella and Susannah gave one another rather amused looks.

"You said you were also given dancing lessons before this evening?" Amelia asked.

"Oh, well, yes," I said. "I explained to Miss Elizabeth that I knew very little of balls or the etiquette required to attend them, and she was all too happy to explain them to me." I laughed, touching a gloved hand to my heart. "It was the most endearing thing. Miss Brown set aside some of her lesson time for her to take the role of the instructor. She proceeded to teach me how to dance, how to carry oneself, and even gave me a brief explanation of all the guests that would be in attendance. Miss Brown found it highly amusing, as did I, though I must admit that I learned a great deal. She is a very well informed young lady."

There were many guests in attendance at the ball, and I could not remember the last time I was witness to so many fine young ladies and gentlemen. Everyone seemed so happy, as well, smiling at one another, laughing heartily.

Across the room, my eyes fell on Mr. Thorne and Miss Elizabeth, who were standing along the wall greeting the last few guests who were somewhat late in arriving. Mr. Thorne carried himself with an air of composure, certainly a man who was capable of throwing a ball as lovely as this one and able to still meet with every guest in turn.

"What of the other servants?" Amelia asked me. "Were they very hard on you for attending the ball as a guest?"

"Not outwardly, no," I said. "Though there were a few who were having a difficult time looking me in the eye these last few days. I certainly do not pretend to be unaware of the fact that it is rather strange for a member of the staff to attend the ball. I imagine they are all discussing it when I am not around."

"Oh, do not fear, sister," Isabella said. "Who

knows? Perhaps you will meet a man here who will win your heart and take you away from this place."

"Or perhaps she has already captured the attentions of the man of the house, and he will be the one to try and win her heart," Susannah said.

"Susannah," Amelia said, scolding her. "You should not say such things when there is a chance you could be overheard."

Susannah gave me a sheepish sort of smile, yet I noticed how she did not apologize.

"Father certainly seems to be enjoying himself," I said, hoping to divert attention. I shifted my gaze to the other side of the room where he stood with Lady Hayward and her husband. Even from where I stood, I could see that she was introducing him to a great many people. I could see, even from here, that she was being very amiable.

Father had done his best to find a proper suit to wear, and as kind and as personable as he was, I knew it would not be difficult for him to leave a lasting, positive impression on everyone he met.

"It certainly was very kind of Mr. Thorne to invite us all to his ball," Amelia said. "I am grateful to him."

"As am I," Isabella said. "Juliana, you must tell him so."

"And I shall, when he is not otherwise occupied," I said.

There was a stirring on the other side of the room, and the sound of something striking the side of a glass.

We all turned to see Mr. Thorne standing beside the entrance into the ballroom, his hands raised, a spoon clinking delicately against the crystal flute in his hand.

"Ladies and gentlemen, I would like to welcome you all to Northington Park, and to a ball that I am throwing in honor of my dear daughter, Miss Elizabeth."

There was clapping and laughter. Everyone knew she was too young to be coming out into society, but that did not mean that she wanted to miss any of the excitement that her father would be enjoying.

"I should like to open the ball with a dance and would encourage you all to join in soon after," he said.

His head turned, and his eyes fell upon me. Even though I was halfway across the room from him, I knew that his gaze had fallen upon me.

"Musicians, if you would be so kind," he said.

From the opposite side of the room, music began

to play from violins and cellos. Couples began to come together, their hands joining as they began to walk toward the center of the room together.

"I wonder if anyone will ask me to dance," Susannah said, gazing around the room. "There certainly are enough agreeable men here."

"Well, I believe our eldest sister will be the first one asked to dance," Amelia said, her eyes fixed on a person in the distance.

I turned to follow her gaze, and found Mr. Thorne making his way toward us.

"Oh, heavens, no," I said, shaking my head. "He is not coming this way. He must be going to speak with another one of the young women here. Why would he—"

"Good evening, Miss Honeyfield."

My heart leapt into my throat, and I slowly turned to see Mr. Thorne standing behind me, smiling down at me.

He looked exceedingly handsome tonight; his coat was a deep, rich grey, like the sky just before the dawn's early light. His hair was swept back out of his face, allowing his blue-green eyes to be seen very clearly in the warm light of the ballroom. His smile was broad and genuine, and it was directed at me.

"Mr. Thorne," I said, my face flushing pink. "How do you do?" I asked, dipping into a curtsy.

"I am well, thank you very much," he said, bowing to me as well.

Susannah giggled beside me.

"And how are you ladies enjoying the evening?" he asked, looking back and forth between my sisters.

"Oh, very well, sir," Amelia said.

"Yes, indeed," Isabella said. "You are too kind to invite us, sir."

"We appreciate your hospitality, sir," Susannah said. "We are indebted to you."

"I am pleased to hear that you all are happy," he said. "Your eldest sister has been preparing for the ball all week, hoping to make it the very best that she could for you."

All three sisters turned to look at me, their eyes widening.

"So, Miss Honeyfield. Would you care to dance this first dance with me?" he asked.

I stared at him, infinitely surprised. "Sir? Do you mean it?"

"Well, of course," he said. "I would not have you sit along the wall all evening. It would be a shame to let such a pretty dress go to waste. Wouldn't you agree?"

I could not believe that he had asked me, and for the first dance, no less.

He held out his hand to me, smiling. "It would be my honor," he said.

All three of my sisters were staring at me, waiting for my response.

Slowly, I lifted my hand and settled it into his palm. "Very well," I said. "I would be quite happy to."

I heard my sisters murmuring to one another as Mr. Thorne lead me away, toward the center of the room. As we went, I could sense the others in the room turning their attentions toward us. I wondered what my father must have thought. I wondered what my Aunt Patience must have thought.

All these guests who had never seen me before were likely wondering who I was, catching the eye of such a prestigious man. The host, no less, the man who owned the home in which the ball was being held.

"That dress looks magnificent on you," Mr. Thorne said as we reached the others, taking our place among them.

"Thank you very much," I said. Part of me wished to express how unworthy I felt about wearing such an exquisite gown or how I was not fit to wear it in the first place, but I held my tongue. There was no need to cause a scene in the middle of our dance. It was best for me to swallow my concerns until later. I would certainly have a chance to tell him how I felt after the ball was over.

"And are you enjoying yourself like your sisters?" Mr. Thorne asked.

"Of course," I said. "This is one the most exciting evenings of my life, sir."

"I am pleased to hear it," he said.

We danced for some time, and I was doing my best to keep up. The dances were a little more complicated than ones I had danced as a child, and I was infinitely grateful for Miss Elizabeth's help to teach me. After a few nervous moments, I found myself looking up at Mr. Thorne more than at my own feet, content at being able to simply follow his lead.

As we danced, we talked about simple things, things that would be appropriate for a master and his daughter's tutor to speak of. Innocent matters, and soon they became more familiar. We talked about Miss Elizabeth and of matters concerning others in the home. As we spoke, though, I realized he gave no indication to those around us that I worked for him; he made it seem as if I simply was very familiar with the goings on at Northington Park.

For the time being, I allowed myself the simplicity of pretending as if I were his cousin, or perhaps an old acquaintance, and he seemed pleased to oblige.

In those moments, I was struck with a stark truth. This is what I would feel if I were not simply a tutor for his daughter. If my life had been different, then perhaps Mr. Thorne and I would have met at a ball just like this one. Perhaps he would have smiled at me, and I would have blushed like I was.

There were many in my life who attempted to sway my feelings toward Mr. Thorne. I believed they were seeing more than was truly happening. I thought his kindness was nothing more than good will. And yet, I could not deny that his actions toward me were very different than how he treated the rest of his staff. It wasn't as if he did not care for them, but it was as if he had seen something different in me from the beginning.

My sisters' words stayed with me as I danced with him. How many men would go with their daughter's tutor to her sister's bedside, as well as sending for a physician at such last minute? It seemed so obvious now.

But... Was it all right? Was it good for me to open my heart to this man who, in truth, I hardly knew?

No, that was not true, was it? I knew him better than most women knew the men they married. I had the chance to see him in ordinary situations—at breakfast, during holidays... even with children.

He was the only man who had ever taken any sort of interest in me, and if I was honest with myself, I realized that he was also the only sort of man that I would ever want to have taken an interest in me.

For that moment, I was able to forget about my questions about his past and simply enjoy dancing with such a handsome man.

However, those fears were not long laid to rest.

After another dance with Mr. Thorne, he asked if I would be ready to play the pianoforte in the next room where some of the guests had moved to rest. Eager to continue to please him, I agreed.

He set me up at the piano, and at once, all the nervousness I had been feeling came back like a wave, making my face pale and my fingers tremble as I rested them on the keys.

Miss Elizabeth was grinning at me, waiting eagerly for me to play. "You should play our favorite song, Miss Honeyfield!" she said, clapping her hands together. She looked like a proper lady with her silk gloves and dried flowers in her hair.

So play our favorite song I did.

The nervousness went away sooner than I expected it would, and the joy of simply playing took its place.

I sang along with Miss Elizabeth, and soon, it was just as if we were having another lesson.

Soon, though, the songs began to slow. Guests began to move into smaller groups, speaking in low voices to one another.

My music and I blended into the background, and I was perfectly fine with that. It gave me a chance to relax and reflect.

Mr. Thorne was nearby, speaking with a pair of older gentlemen. I noticed, though, that Mr. Thorne's expression was becoming less amiable as they spoke. He nodded his head, his expression grim.

I was not one for overhearing conversations, but as the rest of the room grew quieter, the easier it was for me to catch parts of what the man was saying to him.

"...and I find myself asking the same questions, Mr. Thorne. Why is it that you continue to hide the truth?" the man asked.

"I assure you, Mr. Redford. There is nothing to hide," he said.

The small hairs on the back of my neck stood up, and I fumbled across one of the keys. I recovered quickly, though, not wishing to draw attention to myself. I faded out the song I played for one I could play without much thought.

"Surely, I cannot be the only one who finds the circumstances rather suspicious," Mr. Redford said. "Even after all this time, I am not the only one who wonders precisely what happened that night."

Mr. Thorne let out a heavy sigh. "Mr. Redford, I assure you—"

"Do not pretend, Mr. Thorne. I am well aware of your secret. Do you still deny it?" Mr. Redford asked.

Mr. Thorne hesitated. "No," he said. "No, I suppose I can deny it no longer."

"Then you admit to it," Mr. Redford said. "You admit that what happened was your fault?"

"Yes, Mr. Redford, I do," Mr. Thorne said.

I realized it had been several moments since I had stopped playing.

My heart was hammering in my ears, and I felt as if the room was closing in around me.

"Miss Honeyfield?" Mr. Thorne asked.

I looked up, seeing Mr. Thorne staring at me, rather perplexed.

"I…" I began. "I'm terribly sorry, sir, please excuse me."

I rose from the bench and hurried from the room.

Fear coursed through my veins as I ran from the ballroom, making my way to the stairwell. I needed to get away from the people. I needed some space. I needed to think.

I found myself dashing down the hall toward the school room, carrying my heavy skirts as I did.

When I threw open the door and hurried in, I found Miss Brown in there at her desk.

She leapt to her feet when I came in. "Miss Honeyfield," she said. "Whatever is the matter?"

Gasping for breath, I closed the door behind myself. "I just… I heard… something dreadful, Miss Brown. I do not wish to believe it, I cannot."

"Come sit down," she said, pulling a chair out at the table for me. "It's quite all right."

I took the seat and stared up into her face.

"What has you so agitated?" she asked, sitting down beside me.

I was having trouble collecting my thoughts. It only took me a brief moment to decide to trust Miss

Brown with what I had heard from the other servants. "Have you… heard any rumors about Mr. Thorne?" I asked.

Miss Brown's eyes narrowed. "Miss Honeyfield, you must be very careful with what you are about to say. Surely, you must know this."

"Yes, but I just heard…" I said. "Have you heard the rumors about his brother?"

Miss Brown looked away, but there was clear recognition on her face. "I have heard those rumors, yes," she said. "But I never could have believed them myself."

"Neither could I," I said. "But he was just speaking to a man downstairs, who was accusing him of keeping a secret, something that seemed suspicious that happened years ago."

"It… could have been anything," Miss Brown said. "Did they mention the brother?"

"No," I said. "But you should have heard the tone that Mr. Thorne was using. He was so stern, and there was this look in his eyes."

Miss Brown nodded. "I cannot imagine he would have admitted something so freely in the middle of his ball," she said.

"Neither can I," I said. "Who is Mr. Redford?"

Miss Brown's face turned sour. "A ruthless sort of

man. Someone who would easily look for something like this to blackmail Mr. Thorne with."

That did nothing to ease my fears.

"We must be patient," Miss Brown said. "We cannot make any assumptions. Not yet."

"How, though?" I asked. "I danced with him. How am I to pretend as if I heard nothing?"

"You *must*," Miss Brown said. "And you should return to the ball. It will only draw more suspicion."

I nodded. She was right.

"Do not worry," Miss Brown said. "We shall get through this. Together. We shall find the truth."

"I hope you are right," I said. "I truly, truly do."

15

I had a difficult time sleeping the night after the ball. I did as Miss Brown suggested and made my way back down to the ball after speaking with her in the school room. It was difficult, and I apologized to my sisters, who were apparently quite concerned. I insisted I was fine, that some sort of dizzy spell had come over me and I just needed to rest. Susannah said that it must have been from all the dancing I was doing, and I said nothing to correct her, just laughed with her and my other sisters.

The ball came to an end rather late, and my father and sisters left in the carriages brought by Sir Hayward. They all hugged me and made me promise I would keep them informed about everything going on at Northington Park. I promised I would write as soon as anything interesting happened, hoping against all hope that I could write about something other than what I feared I might have to—that I was being discharged from Mr. Thorne's estate due to his arrest for his brother's murder.

I was deeply unsettled as I made my way toward the school room the next morning. Everyone was quite groggy. Everyone except me.

I jumped at every sound and tried to suppress my fears of silhouettes at the end of the halls. I worried that I would run into Mr. Thorne, and I was certain I was not quite ready to see him yet.

Part of my mind kept insisting that there was no possible way that what I had heard had anything to do with Mr. Thorne's brother, and that I was likely blowing the whole thing out of proportion. Yet, there was another part of me that just could not accept that entirely. Something prevented me from believing it, and I struggled with it all through the morning.

Miss Brown and I said nothing to one another as we began our days. Miss Elizabeth came in, and Miss Brown began her lessons. I tried to keep focused on what she was teaching, but my thoughts kept wandering.

Soon, it was time for Miss Elizabeth's music lesson. She skipped over to the piano where I sat, waiting for her. "Wasn't last night just wonderful, Miss Honeyfield?" she asked. "I could have danced all night."

I smiled at warmly as I could. "I am certain you would if you could have," I said.

She sat down beside me with a heavy, happy sigh. "I cannot wait to be old enough to dance at balls with handsome young men." She laid her hands on her cheeks, staring dreamily out the window. "I shall be the most beautiful woman at the ball, the girl that every man shall wish to dance with."

"Well, until then, we must continue with our lessons," I said. "Men appreciate an accomplished woman, and wouldn't you like to be able to play the pianoforte for whomever it is that you will give your heart to?"

"Of course," Miss Elizabeth said.

"What is all this talk of giving my dear daughter's heart away?" came an amused question from Mr. Thorne.

My eyes widened, and all the color drained from

my face. I turned on the bench and saw him standing just inside the door, grinning at us.

"Mr. Thorne," Miss Brown said, getting to her feet at once. I followed suit.

"Easy, ladies, it's quite all right," he said. "After all our excitement last night, I am quite struggling to keep my focus on anything I attempt to do today. I thought I should check in on my dear daughter and see if I could catch some of her lesson."

"How wonderful, Father," Miss Elizabeth said. "Isn't that wonderful, Miss Honeyfield?"

"I daresay it is," I said, smiling at her and turning my back to him once more. I took my seat at the bench. "There now, Miss Elizabeth. I think today we shall practice with your scales to warm up. Then, I thought I should teach you a more difficult song."

Her eyes widened. "Truly?"

"Indeed," I said. "But it will require a great deal of concentration. Perhaps you can show your father what you have learned later?"

"Oh, never you mind me," he said, taking a seat in one of the chairs at the school table. "I shall not be in your way."

I smiled, but I found myself growing more nervous by the moment.

After her lesson, Mr. Thorne was speaking with

Miss Brown. I watched her carefully, amazed at how easy it was for her to pretend that nothing was wrong. Perhaps in her mind, there was no need to worry until the news was proved to be true.

"Elizabeth, why don't you go on ahead of me to dinner," he said. "There was something I wanted to discuss with Miss Honeyfield."

My face flooded with color as I stared down at the sheet music I was reorganizing. I paused, fear coursing through me. Whatever could he need to speak with me about?

"All right, Father," Miss Elizabeth said. "Thank you, Miss Brown and Miss Honeyfield."

"You are quite welcome, dear," Miss Brown said.

Mr. Thorne stepped closer to me. "I saw that you seemed quite distressed last night as you were playing," he said. "It concerned me greatly. I hoped that you were not suddenly becoming ill."

"Oh, no, sir, I am quite all right," I said. "It was a dizzy spell, nothing more. I have not had so much excitement in years." That part, at least, was entirely the truth.

"Then I shall call for Dr. Williams," he said. "You certainly do not need to be suffering from the same ailments as your sister was. If I sent a letter, it could be to him by tomorrow, and he could come and see to you."

"No, thank you, Mr. Thorne," I said. "Really, I am quite all right."

"Have you been sleeping all right? Was it too much last night?" he asked.

"No," I said, rather forcefully.

He stared at me.

I gaped at him like a fish out of water. "No, sir. I am quite all right, I assure you."

His eyes narrowed, and he set his hands on his hips. "Miss Honeyfield is something troubling you?" he asked. "You are having a difficult time meeting my eye. It is as if you are ashamed of something."

I looked over at Miss Brown, desperate for her help to assuage this. I was not ready to tell him the truth. I knew that I never would be.

"Miss Honeyfield, I asked you a question," he asked, a bit more firmly.

My heart raced. I was a mouse trapped in a corner.

This man that I had found myself fawning over the night before was very nearly repulsive to me now.

"Mr. Thorne, I fear that you are holding a secret,"

I said. "A detrimental secret that could affect all of those around you."

His eyes narrowed. "A secret? What precisely are you accusing me of?"

Miss Brown shook her head from behind Mr. Thorne's back.

But I knew it was no use. I had already said too much.

I straightened my shoulders and met his gaze as steadily as I could. "Sir, what happened with your brother?" I asked.

He seemed as stunned as I was. "My brother?" he asked. "What, precisely, are you asking of me?"

"Sir, she did not mean anything by it," Miss Brown said, taking a step forward.

"Enough," Mr. Thorne said, glaring at her and then at me. He took another step toward me. "You mention my brother. You speak of the rumors that have no doubt been spoken of me? What have you heard?"

I was no longer wishing to discuss this with him. I was a fool for ever thinking I should say something in the first place. An utter fool.

"I am waiting for an answer, Miss Honeyfield," he said.

"I have heard that your brother met an untimely

demise," I said.

"And?" he asked.

I pursed my lips. I could not bring myself to say it.

"I imagine you meant to say that it was I who ended my brother's life?" he asked. "Am I correct, Miss Honeyfield?"

I was amazed that he had admitted it so readily.

He scoffed, turning away and pacing over toward the window.

"I overheard the conversation with Mr. Redford last night," I said. "I heard him say that he was suspicious of something that happened years ago and suspected that you were attempting to cover up the truth."

He looked over at me. "So, dabbling in gossip as well as eavesdropping? I never would have expected that from you."

"Mr. Thorne, you cannot imagine that any of us would be settled after hearing such things," I said. "How devastated we all have been, wondering if this was the truth."

"And you are telling me that you believe these rumors?" he asked me rather frankly.

"No, sir, of course we don't," Miss Brown said.

"Clearly, Miss Honeyfield has her suspicions," he

said, his brow furrowed. "Which surprises me greatly, as I know her to be one of the most sensible people that I have had the pleasure of knowing."

I dipped my head. To hear such a compliment in such a negative way, it hurt my heart.

"I must tell you, Miss Honeyfield. I am deeply disappointed in your behavior. Your listening in on my conversation is troubling enough, but do you know what troubles me most?" he asked. "After knowing me for as long as you have, how could you possibly accuse me of something like that?"

I was at a loss for how to respond. This was not how I imagined all of this happening.

"And still you have nothing to say for yourself," he said.

"You have not yet contradicted me, sir," I said.

"Must I?" he asked. "It seems that my word is not enough for you to believe me, is it, Miss Honeyfield? It seems that my word is not enough for any of those on my staff."

I swallowed hard, my hands folded in front of myself, attempting to hide their trembling.

"Come with me, Miss Honeyfield," he said, turning on his heels and striding toward the door. "And I shall show you the truth. For I now realize that there is no other way for you to believe me."

16

I knew I had no choice but to follow after him. Fear gripped my heart as I followed him from the school room, our footsteps echoing off the silent halls.

His hands were balled into fists as he walked a few steps ahead of me, his shoulders hunched and tense.

There was no amount of reprimanding of myself that would ever be able to make up for what had happened. And I was well aware that there would never be enough apologies I could make to make him forgive me for what I had said. I had stepped far outside the boundaries established for me, and I would be incredibly fortunate if he would only dismiss me, for I knew he had the power to completely ruin my reputation, and I would be utterly worthless to my father once more.

We turned down a hall I had only ever been down once, and it was a moment before I realized that he was heading for the secret door that he had been so cross that I had seen into that one day.

He stopped before it, pulling a thick, old iron key from the pocket of his coat and sliding it into the lock. He pushed the door open and stood aside, gesturing inside. "You may go in," he said.

I blinked at him. "Sir, I—"

"Please," he said, and I realized that a great deal of his anger had faded. Instead, I saw sorrow in his eyes.

That, alone, was the reason I found myself stepping across the threshold.

I found myself in a rather small room. His study was much larger. A narrow fireplace sat along the wall, and shelves were along every wall. There was a single chair in the room, and a small, round table beside it.

It reminded me of a rather small receiving room, yet I knew that he had likely never received any guests here in the first place.

"Tell me, Miss Honeyfield, what do you see?" he asked.

I stared around, my heart catching in my throat. I saw many of the same things I had seen the first time, including the military jacket, as well as the saber and the extensive collection of books.

"These are all my brother's belongings," he said, crossing the room to examine a portrait on the wall. I had not noticed it when I came in.

The man in the painting was very familiar to me, though there were a few slight differences. The man in the painting was broader in the shoulders, and his nose was larger. He wore facial hair, and his brow seemed furrowed more naturally than Mr. Thorne's.

He sighed heavily, looking around the room. "That coat that hangs on the wall was mine, what I was meant to wear in the military. It belonged to my father, once, and so I was to inherit the family task of entering the military as the second son."

He pointed to the saber. "That was my brother's, presented to him by our uncle when he came of age. It has the Thorne name inscribed on the hilt. It was always meant to be his, worn for ceremony, so I hung it here so that I can always honor him when I see it."

He looked toward the shelf.

"I have many things of his. Toys from his childhood, his hunting rifle... even his favorite carved box that our parents had brought home for him on their trip to London. He used to keep his pens and other small trinkets in it when he was younger."

"Sir," I said. "Why did you bring me in here?" I asked.

"To show you that I have grieved the loss of my brother every day since he died," he said. "To prove to you that I loved him dearly, and that I would never have been able to take his life."

He pulled one of the books from the shelf, flipping it open. I caught sight of a name scribbled across the front page. *Andrew Thorne.*

"It was a foggy day," he said, staring down at the name. "We were out hunting pheasants with our father. My brother and I decided to stay out longer, even though we knew that it would be much harder to see. We were just happy to be out together."

He tucked the book back onto the shelf and turned his attention to me, his eyes somber.

"We were not at home here but instead were visiting our cousins. We were unfamiliar with the landscape, and with the fog, it was quite easy to miss a step or catch one's foot on a root. He and I became separated from the others, but we trusted that the fog would lift and we would be able to make it home without error."

I found I was holding my breath and could see that this was a story he had not told for many, many years.

"There was a cliff. We could not see it. The edge appeared before we even knew it was there, and my brother, he... he could not stop. His foot slipped, and he stumbled off the side. I reached out and grabbed him, but the fog made our hands slick, and he was much heavier than I was, being so much older," he said.

He put his hands on his hips, attempting to steady himself.

"I could not pull him up. He slipped. I was unable to catch him," he said, his voice low and dark. "All I could do was kneel there and cry like a child. I wasn't even able to see his face as he fell."

I swallowed hard. What a terrible way for someone he loved to die.

"I made my way back to the house, though I am still uncertain how. My father asked me about my brother, and I... I couldn't bring myself to tell him." He swallowed hard. "They found his body later in the day. He had not survived the fall. Everyone asked me what happened. My cousins assumed we were fighting, just as they would have, and no matter how much I insisted it wasn't true, no one seemed to believe me."

I looked up into the face of Mr. Thorne's brother. He was a dignified looking man with strong, handsome features and a whole life ahead of him that he would never be able to live.

"My mother never forgave me for what happened," he said. "I think she believed me to be guilty for what happened. I don't think she thought I had been malicious and pushed him, but I think she blamed me for not saving him when I had the chance to. And it was something I have regretted every day since, myself."

He looked around the room.

"I have set my brother's things in this room as a way to try and lock away all of my unhappy memories," he said.

"Mr. Thorne," I said. "I... I cannot begin to apologize for the way I have acted. I had no idea that you were so pained by this burden. You are absolutely right. I should have known better, should have trusted you without fail."

"I cannot blame you for listening to the rumors spread by the servants," he said. "My mother certainly was not quiet about her own suspicions. It seems it has followed me, though I had been almost certain I was rid of it permanently."

"What of your conversation with Mr. Redford?" I asked. "Did he learn of your brother's death?"

Mr. Thorne's face was colored with confusion for a moment. "Oh, you mean our conversation last night at the ball? No, that had nothing to do with my brother. In fact, he seemed to discover that I was the one behind the surprise party we had thrown for him so many years ago. He is very adverse to those sorts of events, as they cost a great deal of money that he was unaware of spending. His wife, though, wanted to do something nice for his birthday. He has been seeking the supporter of that party for some time. I was surprised he had finally traced it back to me."

I breathed a sigh of great relief. "Mr. Thorne, I truly am sorry for believing you to be capable of something so horrific. But, if I may be honest, I never truly believed it. Not fully. Mr. Redford's words simply frightened me, and I was very mistaken."

"I understand," he said. "I imagine I would feel the same if I were in your place."

I bowed my head. "Sir, I shall understand if you would wish to dismiss me at your earliest convenience," I said. "It should not take me more than an hour or two to collect my belongings, and I could carry my suitcase back to my father's house, and—"

"Dismiss you?" he asked. "That is the very last thing I wish to do, Miss Honeyfield. While I was disappointed at your lack of trust in me, upon reflection, I can understand why you might have thought the way you had about me. And, if I am honest, I am rather impressed with your lack of fear in confronting me."

"You are mistaken, sir, I was quite afraid indeed," I said. "I was a fool for ever attempting to pull the truth from you. I was out of place, and it was wrong."

"Miss Honeyfield, I never wish for you to stop seeking the truth about me," he said, so suddenly, so starkly that it caught me off guard.

I stared at him, my heart beginning to race. "What?"

"I have realized for some time now that Northington Park is in need of a lady. Not only the estate, but I have been without a wife for too long. My dear Elizabeth needs a mother. When your aunt, Lady Hayward, came to me and spoke of your qualities, at once I imagined what you must be like. I was uncertain as to whether you were the sort to marry or not, so I hired you with the hope of getting to know you. Not only have you impressed and bewitched my daughter, but you have entranced me as well, Miss Honeyfield. I have found myself longing to have you near me, to see your lovely face each day. To hear my daughter speak so highly of you fills my heart with joy."

"But sir," I said. "I am nothing. I am a poor daughter of a poor clergyman, and I have nothing to offer you."

"You have a great deal to offer me, Miss Honeyfield. Your sensibility, your affection, your care of my daughter... There is no woman I would rather ask to marry me, Miss Honeyfield. Not a woman I have met who can surpass the standards that you have so easily created in my heart. In truth, I fear that I will not be worthy of you—your kindness, your value of others, your love for your family."

My heart was pounding so quickly that I could hear it in my ears.

"When we danced last night, I had made up my mind," Mr. Thorne said, taking a step toward me. "I care not what others may think. I have fallen in love with you, despite your position, despite your background. That matters not when you are such a woman of great value, irreplaceable in my opinion. And I cannot live another moment with you under the same roof as I, not knowing whether or not you shall have me. For I leave the choice to you."

I stared into his face, and all the feelings I had come to recognize the night before came flooding back to me. The hope, the joy, the sight of what could be a very happy future.

"You are the only sort of man that I could ever accept," I said, a smile appearing on my face. "I had convinced myself I would never marry, and then you and your thoughtfulness gave me great hope that I dared not believe."

"So, you will have me?" he asked, his eyes widening. His lovely, blue-green eyes.

I nodded. "Yes, Mr. Thorne. I shall have you."

He stepped forward, and for a moment, I could only stare into his eyes.

Then he took my hand in his and knelt down onto one knee.

"Then I promise to be the most devoted husband I can be."

I laughed, despite the seriousness of his tone.

He grinned at me. "Imagine what my daughter will say to this."

"Our daughter, you mean," I said. That was certainly going to take some getting used to.

Now available!
A Perilous Secret: Secrets of the Honeyfield Sisters: Book 2

Made in the USA
Las Vegas, NV
24 January 2022